"We'll be the only occup.... ...., added.

Rory swallowed at the low, sexy note in his voice. She'd be alone with Mac, on a Caribbean island with warm, clear water and white beaches and palm trees. Utterly and absolutely alone. She wasn't sure whether the appropriate response was to be thrilled or terrified. Or both.

Sex and business don't mix, she told herself. *He's your patient!*

Sun, sea, sexy island...sexy man.

Not liking the cocky look in his eyes, the glint that suggested that he knew exactly what she was thinking about, she lifted her nose. "Well, at least we won't disturb the neighbors with your screams of pain when we start physio."

"Or your screams of pleasure when I make you fall apart in my arms," Mac replied without a second's hesitation.

Rory's heart thumped in her chest but she kept her eyes locked on his, refusing to admit that he rattled her. That instead of making her furious, as it should, her entire body was humming in anticipation and was very on board with that idea.

Rory folded her arms and rocked on her heels. "I hate it when you say things like that."

"No, you don't. You hate it because it turns you on."

* * *

Trapped with the Maverick Millionaire is part of the From Mavericks to Married series—Three superfine hockey players finally meet their matches!

Dear Reader,

Trapped with the Maverick Millionaire is the first in my new series called From Mavericks to Married, and I am so excited to introduce you to Mac McCaskill, Kade Webb and Quinn Rayne, all professional ice hockey players for the Vancouver Mavericks. All single, all playing the field, all determined to *keep* playing the field...

While Kade and Quinn have hung up their skates to become the CEO and acting coach of the Mavericks respectively, Mac McCaskill is still playing professionally and he is the captain of the wildly popular franchise. When the owner of the Mavericks dies, the three friends put their plans to buy the franchise from the widow into motion, but they are facing stiff opposition from other interested parties. It's a sensitive time for the Mavericks and they can't afford for anything to go wrong.

So when the very independent, hates-to-ask-for-help Mac injures his shoulder, the friends rally to keep his career-threatening injury under wraps and they recruit the best physiotherapist in the Northwest to help him regain his strength.

Unfortunately, that physiotherapist is Rory Kydd, the sister of the model Mac publicly humiliated years before and the girl he almost kissed shortly thereafter. Rory doesn't want to work with Mac, either. Their attraction is still off the charts, but he makes her an offer she can't refuse.

Happy reading!

With love,

Joss

Connect with me at josswoodbooks.com

Twitter: @JossWoodBooks

Facebook: Joss Wood Author

JOSS WOOD

TRAPPED WITH THE MAVERICK MILLIONAIRE

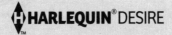

Recycling programs
for this product may
not exist in your area

ISBN-13: 978-0-373-73467-2

Trapped with the Maverick Millionaire

Copyright © 2016 by Joss Wood

Printed in U.S.A.

Joss Wood's passion for putting black letters on a white screen is only matched by her love of books and traveling (especially to the wild places of southern Africa) and, possibly, by her hatred of ironing and making school lunches.

Joss has written over sixteen books for the Harlequin KISS, Harlequin Presents and, most recently, Harlequin Desire lines.

After a career in business lobbying and local economic development, Joss now writes full-time. She lives in KwaZulu-Natal, South Africa, with her husband and two teenage children, surrounded by family, friends, animals and a ridiculous amount of books.

Joss is a member of the RWA (Romance Writers of America) and ROSA (Romance Writers of South Africa).

Books by Joss Wood

Harlequin Desire

Taking the Boss to Bed

From Mavericks to Married

Trapped with the Maverick Millionaire

Harlequin Kiss

The Last Guy She Should Call
Flirting with the Forbidden
More than a Fling?

Harlequin Presents

One Night, Two Consequences
Her Boss by Day...
Behind the Headlines

Visit her Author Profile page at Harlequin.com, or josswoodbooks.com, for more titles.

To the "Book Sisters," Romy Sommers, Rae Rivers and Rebecca Crowley. All are fantastic authors but are also funny, supportive and kind.

Basically, you rock!

Prologue

Rory Kydd, dressed in a too-small T-shirt and battered pajama bottoms, walked into the kitchen of her sister's luxurious kitchen and looked at the dark screen of the TV sitting on the counter.

Her best friend, Troy, had texted to tell her the Vancouver Mavericks had won and there had been high drama during the post-game interview. She was tempted to turn on the TV to see what he was talking about but, because she had a paper due and exams looming—and because she was trying not to think about one Maverick player in particular—she decided to have a cup of coffee and go back to the books. But even if she didn't give in to temptation, it couldn't be denied, team newbies Kade Webb, Quinn Rayne and Mark "Mac" McCaskill were a handful both on and off the ice, and Vancouver had three new heroes.

Three young, unfairly talented and, it had to be said, stupidly good-looking heroes.

And the best-looking of the bunch, in her opinion, was dating her older sister Shay.

Rory poured herself a cup of coffee and leaned her butt against the counter. Shay and Mac made perfect sense, she told herself. Again. Shay was a model and a TV presenter. Mac was the supertalented, superfine center for the city's beloved hockey team. They were the perfect age, she was twenty-three and Mac a year older, and, according to the press, because they were both beautiful and successful, a perfect match.

It was all perfectly perfect.

Except that Rory wasn't convinced.

And that wasn't because Mac made her toes tingle and her stomach jump. It had nothing to do with her insane attraction to the man. No, she'd spent enough time around Shay and Mac to see the cracks in their relationship, to know the bloom was off the rose and Shay was acting like a loon. Judging by Mac's wary, closed-off expression whenever Rory saw them together, Shay had him on the Crazy Express.

Rory would bet her last dollar Shay was feeling desperate, calling and texting relentlessly whenever they were apart. Since they both had such demanding careers, they were apart *a lot*.

Rory knew why Shay was insecure, why she couldn't trust a man. Rory had grown up in the same house as Shay. The difference between them was that Shay kept hoping there was one man out there who could be faithful and monogamous.

Rory was pretty damn sure that, like unicorns and the yeti, such a creature didn't exist.

Rory scowled and wrapped her hands around her mug. Shay hadn't told Mac why she was acting crazy, Rory was pretty sure of that. To complicate matters further, Rory and Mac had somehow become friends. Sadly, that was all they could ever be. He was too good-looking, too much of a celebrity, too far out of her league. She was a college student. He was a successful player, both on and off the ice… Oh, and that other little thing—*he was her sister's boyfriend!*

Besides all that, Mac treated Rory as he would a younger sister. He teased her, argued with her and made her laugh. So she'd caught him watching her with a brooding look on that sexy face once or twice but she wasn't an idiot, she knew it didn't mean anything. He'd probably wanted to talk to her about Shay, wanted advice on how to deal with her volatility. Rory *never* wanted to have that conversation.

A couple of nights ago, he'd given her a lift home from work and she'd been surprised when he didn't mention Shay. Why he'd waited for Rory to finish her waitressing shift was still a mystery but sitting in his sports car, shoulder to shoulder, saying next to nothing, had been the best twenty minutes of her life.

He'd walked her to the door of her lousy apartment building—the same building that currently had no heat— and he'd stood there looking down at her. Something in his expression had heat swirling in her stomach; he'd looked like a man about to kiss a woman. But she knew that had to be her imagination working overtime. He was dating Shay, tall, slim, stunning.

But, just for a moment, she'd thought he'd wanted to kiss her, to taste her, to yank her into his arms… Rory sighed. It wasn't possible. He was dating her sister. He was permanently off-limits; messing in Shay's relationship was a line she would not cross. Thinking about Mac, like that, was a flight of fancy she had no right to take. Enough of that now.

Rory heard the front door open and she waited for Shay's yell that she was home. It didn't come, and Rory heard heavy footsteps on the wooden floor, a tread that couldn't possibly belong to her sister. The saliva in her mouth dried up and her heart rolled; there was only one other person who had a key to Shay's apartment and he was the one person Rory didn't want to be alone with.

In her pajamas, with crazy hair, sans makeup and bra-less.

Mac appeared in the doorway to the kitchen, scowled at her and ran a hand over his tired face. He had a light bruise on his jaw—he'd obviously traded blows on the ice—and the beginnings of a black eye but his injuries looked superficial. It was the emotion she saw in his dark eyes that held her rooted to the spot; he looked frustrated and wound up.

"Where's your sister?" he demanded, his deep, rough voice rumbling over her skin.

"Hello to you too." Rory shrugged and his frown deepened at her response. "I have no idea where she is. Are you okay?"

Mac let out a low, humorless laugh. "Hell, no, I'm screwed." He scowled at her and placed his hands on his hips. "Why are you here?"

"Heat's out in my apartment. Shay said I could sleep here so I don't freeze."

"Just my friggin' luck," Mac muttered.

"Jeez, what's your problem?" Rory asked him as he shrugged out of his expensive leather jacket and tossed it onto the granite counter. A long-sleeved black T-shirt clung to his broad chest and fell, untucked, over well-fitting jeans. He looked hot and tired and so damn sexy she could jump him right now, right where he stood.

Sister's boyfriend, she reminded herself as he walked over to the fridge, pulled out a microbrewed beer and cracked the top. He took a long swallow, sighed and, closing his eyes, placed the bottle against his forehead.

"Bitching, horrible, freakin' revolting day."

She wouldn't have thought the big badass of the Mavericks could sound so melodramatic. "It couldn't have been that dire—you won the game."

Mac's ink-blue eyes lasered into hers. "Did you watch?" he asked, his question as pointed as a spear tip.

Rory shook her head. "Nah, had to study. Why?"

"Because I was wondering why my head was still attached to my neck."

Rory narrowed her eyes. "What did you do?"

Instead of answering, he gave her a long look. Then he placed his bottle on the center island and walked toward her. He gripped the counter, one hand on either side of her body. He was like a big human cage, she thought.

Up close and personal, she could see the slight tinge of auburn in his stubble, notice how long his eyelashes were, could see a faded scar on his top lip. And man, he smelled so good. She wanted to stand on her toes and kiss that scar, run her lips over that bruise on his jaw, kiss his eye better.

*Sister's boyfriend, sister's boyfriend…*she had no right to be standing this close to Mac, tasting his breath, feeling his heat. Playing with fire, coloring outside the lines was something her father did, his worst trait, yet despite that sobering thought she couldn't make herself move away, was unable to duck under Mac's arm. Even though Mac belonged to Shay, Rory wanted just one kiss from him. She wanted to know what he tasted like, how strong his arms felt around her, how it felt to be plastered against that solid wall of muscle. *Just one kiss*...

Gray eyes clashed with blue as his mouth hovered above hers. As she stood there, *so* close and *so* personal, she knew exactly what he'd do, how she'd feel...

His lips would slide across hers, cool, strong...smart. She'd open her mouth to protest, to say they couldn't do this—or to let him in, who knew—and he wouldn't hesitate. As his tongue slid into her mouth, his hand on her lower back would pull her into him and his other hand would delve beneath the elastic of her flannel bottoms to cup a butt cheek. His kiss would turn deeper and wetter and her hands would burrow under his loose T-shirt and explore the muscles of his back, his shoulders, his fabulously ripped stomach.

She'd think that it was wrong but she wouldn't be able to stop herself. Mac would, ever so slowly, pull her T-shirt up to expose her too-small breasts and she'd whimper into his mouth and push her hips against him, needing to rub herself against his hard, hard erection. He'd be what a man felt like, strong, hot, in control...

"I just saw our entire kiss in your eyes. God, that was so hot," Mac growled, and she tasted his sweet breath on her lips again.

"We can't, it's wrong." Rory pushed the words up her throat, past her teeth, through her lips. Four words and she felt like she'd run a marathon.

Mac's eyes stayed locked on hers and, in case she missed the desire blazing there, his erection nudging her knee let her know how much he wanted her. Mac wanted her…he really did. Tall, built, smelling great, gorgeous… how was she supposed to resist him?

Sister's boyfriend, sister's boyfriend…

Rory placed her hands on his pecs and pushed. Mac stepped back but as he did, he lifted his hand to run his knuckle over her cheek. That small, tender action nearly shattered her resolve and she had to grab the edge of the counter with both hands to keep from launching herself into his arms, wrapping her legs around his hips and feasting on that fallen-angel mouth.

So this was primal lust, crazy passion. She wasn't sure she liked how out of control it made her feel. Squirmy, hot, breathless…it was intensely tempting to throw caution to the wind and get lost in the moment. Did having such a flammable reaction to Mac mean that she was more like her dad than she thought? Ugh. This wasn't going to happen, she decided. From this point on she would not kiss, touch or think about her sister's boyfriend. This stopped. Now.

Rory held up a hand. "Back up."

Mac took two steps back and she could breathe. She felt the craziness recede. He jammed his hands into the pockets of his jeans and sent her a brooding look. "That was…"

"Wrong? Crazy? A betrayal of my sister?"

Mac frowned. "Let's not get carried away here. We didn't even kiss."

"We wanted to!"

"But we didn't so let's not get too caught up in the melodrama." Mac picked up his beer, sipped and sighed. His head snapped up and Rory heard the front door closing, heard her sister kicking off her heels. Rory tried to keep her face blank but she felt like her brain and heart were on fire as guilt and shame pricked her skin.

We didn't actually kiss but I really, really wanted to...

"You're here." Shay tossed the words at Mac as she stepped into the kitchen. Rory frowned. Shay didn't walk up to Mac and kiss him. It was what she did, every single time she saw him, whether they'd been apart five minutes or five weeks.

Mac made no effort to touch Shay either. He just stood there wearing that inscrutable face Rory knew he used when he wanted to avoid a scene.

But a scene, she knew it like she knew her own signature, was what they were about to have. Why?

Rory turned her eyes to her sister's face. She recognized that expression, a mixture of betrayal, broken trust, hurt and humiliation. God, she looked devastated.

"What the hell, Mac?" Shay's shout bounced off the walls.

Rory's gaze jumped around the room. How could Shay know? Did she have cameras in the apartment? X-ray vision? A girlfriend's gut instinct?

Mac held his hands up. "I'm sorry, Shay, for all of it. I never meant to hurt you."

"Yet you're doing such a fine job of it." Shay wiped her eyes with the back of her wrist. "There were easier ways to get rid of me, Mac. You didn't have to humiliate me on national TV."

Rory looked at Mac and then at Shay. Okay, maybe this conversation had nothing to do with Rory and the almost-kiss. "What are you talking about? What did he do?"

Shay let out a laugh that held absolutely no amusement. "You haven't seen it?"

"Seen what?"

Shay's laugh was brittle. "Well, you're probably the only person in the city—the country—who hasn't!" She lunged for the remote on the counter and jabbed her finger on the buttons to get the TV to power up. While she flipped through channels, Rory snuck a look at Mac. He gripped the bridge of his nose with his finger and thumb and he looked utterly miserable.

Sad, sorry and, to be frank, at the end of his rope.

"And in today's sports news, Maverick's center Mac McCaskill was caught on an open mic commenting on sex, monogamy and hot women."

Rory snapped her head up and looked at the screen. Footage of the post-match news appeared on the screen. Quinn, Kade and Mac lounged behind a table draped with the Maverick's logo. Kade said something that was too low to hear and the three of them laughed.

"The blonde reporter in the third row is seriously hot." Quinn's voice was muffled and she could just hear his words.

"Did you see the redhead?" Kade demanded, his voice equally muted. "I have a thing for redheads."

"You have a thing for all women." Mac's voice was clear and loud; obviously his was the only microphone that was live. Oh…shoot.

"Like you do. When are you going to give up this relationship BS and start playing the field again?" Quinn demanded. "It's not like you're particularly happy with your ball and chain."

"I'm not and you're right, monogamy sucks," Mac said, looking past Quinn. Rory recognized that smile, the appreciation in his eyes. "Your blonde from the third row is very hot."

"Shay is also hot," Kade pointed out.

"Yeah but she's crazy. Besides, I'm bored with tall and built. I'm thinking that petite might be a nice change of pace— Why is Vernon gesturing to me to shut up?"

Then a rash of swear words was followed by: "My mic is on!"

Rory looked at Shay, who'd dropped into a chair at the kitchen table with a vacant look in her eyes. She'd stopped crying and she looked like she'd checked out, mentally and emotionally. Mac picked up his jacket from the counter and walked over to stand in front of Shay. He bent his knees so he could look directly into her face.

"I'm sorry I spoke behind your back and I'm so sorry that I hurt you, Shay. It wasn't my intention. I take full responsibility for running my mouth off. Not my finest moment and I *am* very sorry."

When Shay looked through him and didn't respond, he slowly stood up and placed his apartment key on the counter. Rory looked at her broken, desperately sad sister, grabbed Mac by the arm and pulled him into the hall, feeling as if her gray eyes must be full of angry lightning.

When their eyes met, he lifted one broad shoulder. "Told you I was screwed," he said.

"So you came over here to screw me?" she demanded, thinking about that almost-kiss, fury clogging her throat.

Mac's flashing eyes met hers. "Believe it or not, I'm not that much of a bastard. I didn't even know you would be here."

"What were you thinking, Mac?" she demanded, insanely angry. On behalf of her sister, but also because Rory had trusted him just as Shay had. "You've done so many interviews, you know how mics work."

"I wasn't thinking, dammit!"

Red dots appeared in front of Rory's eyes. "Did you plan this? Was the smack talk an easy way to get out of your relationship with Shay?"

"Contrary to the evidence, I am better than that."

Rory snorted. "You could've fooled me. First you insult my sister, then you almost kiss me? What was *that* about?"

Mac let out a harsh, angry breath. "I knew when I left that news conference that I was toast. I regret what I said. I came here to apologize to Shay but found you instead—"

"So you were angry and frustrated and I was there, a handy way to let off some steam!" Rory interrupted.

Mac's curses filled the small hallway.

Rory drilled a finger into his chest. "How many times have you cheated on Shay? Because that move with me was far too practiced to be your first time!" The red dots turned scarlet and her chest tightened.

Mac stepped back and anger sparked in his eyes. "I'm only going to say this once. I never cheated on your sister. And, babe, you wanted to kiss me as much as I wanted to kiss you! I'll take full responsibility for being a prick on national television but I *will not* take *all* the blame for what almost happened in there."

Guilt swamped her. She knew he was right and she hated it. She didn't want to shoulder *any* of the blame; it would be a lot easier if she could just blame him for everything: for being too sexy, for making her want something she had no right to want.

Mac raked his fingers through his hair. "Look, why don't we let this situation settle down and I'll call you? We can have coffee, chat. Sort this out?"

Pick up where we left off?

That wasn't going to happen. There was no way she could date someone who'd dated—*slept with*—her sister, who'd almost cheated on her. Someone who'd made Rory so crazy with lust that she'd almost betrayed her sister! He would've kissed her had she not stopped him. He would've cheated...of that she was categorically convinced.

She could never trust him.

Ever.

"Don't bother. I'm not interested." Rory walked around him, yanked open the front door and gestured for him to leave. "Go. You've created enough havoc for one evening, for one lifetime."

Mac, with a final inscrutable look, walked out of the Kydd sisters' lives. *Good riddance*, Rory thought. The last thing either of them needed was a cheating, back-stabbing man in their lives.

Rory turned and saw her sister standing in the kitchen doorway. She'd heard every word of their conversation. So she'd stopped the kiss. That meant little. The truth remained: she wanted Shay's man, wanted him badly. They both knew she was more like their dirtbag father than either of them had thought possible. Shay was going to strip layers of skin off her and Rory deserved it.

"You two almost kissed? You had a moment?"

Facing her sister, she couldn't deny the truth. "Yes. I'm really sorry."

"Okay then. Thanks for getting rid of him," Shay told Rory in a cold and hard voice. "Now get the hell out of my apartment and my life."

One

Ten or so years later...

Rory made her way to a small table by the window in the crowded cafeteria of St. Catherine's Hospital, juggling a stack of files, her bag and a large blueberry smoothie. Dumping the files on the table, she took a berry-flavored hit before pulling out a chair and dropping into it. She'd been on the go since before seven, had missed lunch and was now running on fumes. She had two more patients to see. She might be able to get home before eight.

An early night. Bliss.

Her cell phone chimed and Rory squinted at the display, smiling when she saw her sister's name.

"Sorry, something just came up. I'll call you right back," Shay stated before disconnecting.

Rory smiled, grateful that she and Shay were really

close, a minor miracle after the McCaskill incident. Mac running his mouth off and his subsequent breakup with Shay had been the first major media storm involving one of the three most famous Mavericks. It had been the catalyst for the city's fascination with anything to do with Mac, Quinn and Kade.

Shay had been swept up into the madness; she'd been stalked and hassled by reporters and photographers for months. Her life had been a living hell. Unfortunately, because she refused to talk to Rory, Shay had weathered the media attention by herself. She'd lost weight and, as Rory had found out years later, she'd come close to a breakdown. Rory was so grateful the incident was solidly behind them; the man-slut captain of the Mavericks professional ice hockey team was not worth losing sleep, never mind a sister, over.

Except that she did, frequently, still lose sleep thinking about him. Rory sighed. He was her fantasy man, the man she always thought of when she was alone and well, she hated to admit it…horny. She wondered and she imagined and the fact that she did either—both—annoyed the pants off her.

The jerk.

Her cell rang again, Rory answered and Shay said a quick hello. "Sorry, as you picked up the delivery guy arrived."

"No worries, what's up?"

"Dane sent me two dozen red roses."

And, judging by Shay's frantic voice, this was a problem? "Okay, lucky you. Why are you freaking out?"

"Two dozen red roses? Who sends his wife of eight months two dozen red roses? He must be cheating on me."

Here we go again, Rory thought, exasperated. *I haven't*

*had enough coffee to cope with Shay's insecurities.
Thanks again, Dad, for the incredible job you did messing up your daughters' love lives.*

Rory sucked on her straw musing about the fact that
she and Shay had different approaches to life and love.
She was closed off to the idea of handing her heart over
to a man, yet Shay had never given up on love. She had
eventually, she was convinced, caught the last good
guy in the city. The fact that Dane was calm and strong
enough to deal with Shay's insecurities made Rory love
him more.

"He must be having an affair. Nobody can work as
much as he does," Shay fretted.

"Shay! Princess!" Rory interrupted her mumblings.
"Stop obsessing, you're getting yourself into a state.
You're a gorgeous blonde ex-model and you still look
like a million dollars. Dane married you and you promised to trust him."

Shay sighed. "I did, didn't I?"

"Look at your wedding photos. Look at how he's looking at you…like you're the moon and stars and everything
that's perfect." In spite of her cynicism when it came
to romance, Rory couldn't help feeling a little jealous
every time Dane looked at her sister, love blazing from
his eyes. What must it feel like to have someone love you
that much, someone so determined to make you happy?
Logically, she knew the risk wasn't worth it, but…damn,
seeing that look punched her in the heart every time.

"Dane is in the middle of a big case—some gang
shooting, remember? And he's the homicide detective
in charge—and sending you roses is his way of remind-
ing you that he loves you."

"So, no affair?"

"No affair, Shay." And if there was—there wasn't!—but if there was then Rory would take Dane's own weapon and shoot him with it.

Rory said goodbye to her sister, shot off a text to Dane suggesting Shay might need a little extra attention—she and her brother-in-law worked as a team to keep Shay's insecurities from driving them both nuts—and looked down at the folders. She needed to make notes and read over the files of the two patients she was about to see.

She so wanted her own practice. Craydon's Physio-therapy patients were channeled through the system like cans on a conveyor line. There was little time for proper one-on-one care and she was providing patients with only enough treatment to see them through to the next session. Sometimes she wondered if she was doing any good at all.

If she had her own place, she'd slow it down, take more time, do some intensive therapy. But setting up a new practice required cash she didn't have, premises she couldn't afford. She'd just have to keep saving... Maybe one day.

She had barely looked over the first file when her cell rang again. This time it was a number she did not recognize. She answered the call with a cautious hello.

"Rory? Kade Webb, from the Vancouver Mavericks. We met a long time ago."

Kade Webb? Why on earth would he be calling her? "I remember...hi. What can I do for you?"

Kade didn't waste time beating around the bush. "I have a player in St. Catherine's, in The Annex Clinic, and I'd like you to take a look at his chart, assess his injury and tell me what you think."

Rory frowned, thinking fast. "Kade, the Mavericks

have a resident physiotherapist. I know because my bosses would kill for the Mavericks' contract. Why me?"

"Because you have an excellent track record in treating serious sports injuries," Kade replied. "Will you do it? Take a look and let me know what you think?"

"I—"

"Thanks. I'll call you back in a couple of hours."

Rory wanted to tell him that she had patients, that it was against company policy, but he was gone. Argh! She had questions, dammit! Who was the player? What room he was in? Did he know that she was coming? Had Kade spoken to her bosses about this?

Infuriating man, she thought as she stood up and gathered her possessions. It was said that Kade, like his two partners in crime, could charm the dew off roses and the panties off celibates. He hadn't bothered to use any of that charm on her, Rory thought with an annoyed toss of her head.

Not that she would've responded to it, but it would've been nice for him to try.

Mac McCaskill, you stupid idiot, Rory thought.

She'd had many variations of the thought over the past decade, some expressed in language a lot more colorful, but the sentiment was the same. However, this was the first time in nearly a decade that she wasn't mocking his tendency to jump from one gorgeous woman to another or shaking her head over the fact that he was, essentially, a man-slut.

As much as his social life irritated her, she felt sorry for him. He was an exceptionally talented player and as she looked at the notes on his chart, she realized his arm was, to use nontechnical terms, wrecked. For a player of his caliber that was a very scary situation.

"Rory, what are you doing in here?"

Rory, standing next to Mac's bed, flipped a glance over her shoulder and smiled, relieved, when she saw her best friend stepping into Mac's private room. If it had been someone other than Troy she would've had to explain herself.

This was all kinds of wrong, she thought. There were protocols around patient visits and she shouldn't be in Mac's room, looking at his chart, assessing his injury. She should've refused Kade's request, but here she was again, flouting the rules. What was it about McCaskill that made her do that?

"I need to get the mat on him, need to get his circulation restored as soon as possible," she said with urgency.

As a therapist, she wanted the best for him. Even if he was the man who'd hurt her sister. Even if her heart rate still kicked up from just looking at him.

"You're not authorized to treat him and if you're caught we'll both be fired." Troy closed the door behind him, his handsome face creased with worry.

"I'll take full responsibility," Rory retorted. "It's his *arm*, Troy. The arm he needs to slap those pucks into the net at ninety miles an hour."

"Mac usually reaches speeds of a hundred plus miles an hour," Troy, the sports fanatic, corrected her, as she'd counted on him doing.

"Exactly and the mat will start helping immediately," Rory retorted.

"Jobs, fired, on the streets," Troy muttered. Yet he didn't protest when she pulled a mat from her bag and placed the control box it was connected to on Mac's bedside table. When the lights brightened, she very gently wrapped the mat around Mac's injured arm. He didn't stir and Rory relaxed; he was solidly asleep and would be for a while.

Troy was right to worry. Earlier, she'd hesitated and had stood outside of his room, debating whether to go in. Partly because of that almost-kiss years ago, partly because she knew she shouldn't be there, despite Kade's request.

The bottom line was that Mac was a sportsman who needed her expertise and her mat. It was crucial to get his blood flowing through the damaged capillaries to start the healing process. The longer she delayed, the longer he would take to recover. Healing, helping, was what she did, who she was, and she'd fight the devil himself to give a patient what he needed, when he needed it.

Besides, there was little chance of her being discovered in Mac's room. The Annex Clinic was an expensive, private ward attached to St. Catherine's, the hospital situated in the exclusive Vancouver suburb of West Point Gray. Every patient admitted into The Annex had two things in common: they were ridiculously wealthy and they wanted total privacy. Each patient had their own private nurse, and Rory had lucked out because Troy was assigned to room 22.

Not only would he keep her interference a secret, but because he was in the room with her, Rory resisted the urge to run her hand through Mac's thick hair, over his strong jaw shaded with stubble.

He looked as good as he had years ago. Maybe better.

His beard was dark but when he grew it out, it glinted red in the sun. As did his dark brown hair. The corners of his eyes had creases that weren't there a decade ago. He looked, if she ignored his bandaged arm, stronger, fitter and more ripped than he had at twenty-four.

She was a professional, she reminded herself, and she shouldn't be mentally drooling over the man.

"How did you even know he was admitted?" Troy demanded.

"Are you sure he's asleep?" she asked Troy, ignoring his question.

"Morphine. He was in severe pain and it was prescribed." Troy looked at his watch. "Getting back to my point, he only came out of surgery two hours ago and was injured no more than six hours ago. How did you know he was here?"

Rory stood back from the bed and pushed her hands into her lower back as she stretched and explained that Kade, who'd taken on the CEO responsibilities and duties when the owner/manager of the Vancouver Mavericks died, had called and asked her to check on Mac and give her professional opinion.

Troy frowned, worried. "Which is?"

"It's bad, Troy."

Troy swore and Rory knew his disappointment and concern would be shared by most of the residents of Vancouver, Mavericks and Canucks fans alike. Mac was a hell of a player and respected for his leadership and skill. Maverick fans would be devastated to lose their captain for a couple of matches. To lose him for the season would be a disaster. Losing him forever would be a tragedy. But she'd treated enough sport stars to know the impact of his injury, both physical and emotional, would be tremendous.

"How did the surgery go?" Rory asked Troy.

"Good." Troy cleared his throat. "We really could get

fired, Rorks. Even though I know the voodoo blanket helps, it's still a form of treatment and you're not authorized. I like my job."

Rory knew he was right, but she still rolled her eyes at her best friend. "As I've explained to you a million times before, the blanket is not voodoo! It sends electromagnetic signals that stimulate the pumping of the smallest blood vessels. It will help normalize the circulation in this injured area. Kade asked me to be here. He'll work it out. It'll be okay, Troy."

When Troy narrowed his bright green eyes, Rory looked away. "This will run for the next thirty minutes," she said. "Why don't you go get some coffee?"

She needed to be alone with Mac, to get her thoughts—and her reaction to him—under control.

"Ok, I'll be back in thirty."

Troy sent her a worried smile and left the room. When the door closed behind him, she turned back to Mac and couldn't resist the impulse to place her hand on his chest, directly over his heart. Under the thin cotton of the hospital gown she felt the warmth of his skin.

She kept her hand there, trying not to wish she could run it over his hard stomach, down the thick biceps of his uninjured arm. He was so big, his body a testament to a lifetime dedicated to professional sports, to being the hardest, toughest, fastest player on the ice.

She glanced toward the end of the bed at his chart. Reading the chicken scrawl again wouldn't change a damn thing. Essentially, Mac had pulled a tendon partly off the bone and injured a ligament. The surgeons doubted he'd regain his former strength anytime soon, if ever.

That would kill him. Even in the short time they'd known each other, she'd understood that hockey was what

Mac did, who he was. He'd dedicated the last fourteen years to the Mavericks. He was their star player, their leader, the reason fans filled the arena week after week. He was their hope, their idol, the public face of the well-oiled machine Kade managed.

With his crooked smile, his aloof but charming manner and incredible prowess on the ice, he was the city's favorite, regularly appearing in the press, usually with a leggy blonde on his arm. Speculating about when one of the Mavericks Triumvirate—Mac, their captain, Kade as CEO and Quinn as Acting Coach (the youngest in the NHL but widely respected) were all hot and single—would fall in love and settle down was a citywide pastime.

A part of him belonged to the city but Rory doubted that anyone, besides his best friends, knew him. From that time so long ago she knew that Mac, for all his charm, was a closed book. Very little was known about his life before he was recruited to play for the Mavericks. Even Shay hadn't known more than what was public knowledge: he was raised by a single mother who died when he was nineteen, he was a scholarship kid and he didn't talk about his past.

They had that in common. Rory didn't talk about her past either.

Rory adjusted the settings on the control box and Mac shifted in his sleep, releasing a small pain-filled moan. He would hate to know that she'd heard him, she thought. Mac, she remembered, had loathed being sick. He'd played with a broken finger, flu, a sprained ankle, a hurt knee. He'd play through plagues of locusts and an asteroid strike.

Rory looked at his injured arm and sighed. He wouldn't

be able to play through this. How was she supposed to tell Kade that?

A big, hot hand touched her throat and a thumb stroked her jaw. Her brain shut down when he touched her and, just like she had in Shay's kitchen, she couldn't help responding. She allowed her head to snuggle into his hand as he slowly opened his eyes and focused on her face. His fabulous eyes, the deep, dark blue of old-fashioned bottled ink, met hers.

"Hey," he croaked.

"Hey back," Rory whispered, her fingers digging into the skin on his chest. She should remove herself but, once again, she stayed exactly where she was.

So nothing much had changed then. She hadn't grown up at all.

"They must have given me some powerful drugs because you seem so damn real."

Rory shuddered as his thumb brushed over her bottom lip. He thought he was imagining her, she realized.

"Helluva dream… God, you're so beautiful." Mac's hand drifted down her throat over her collarbone. His fingers trailed above the cotton of her tunic to rest on the slight swell of her breast. His eyes, confused and pain-filled, stayed on her face, tracing her features and drinking her in.

Then he heaved in a sigh and the blue deepened to midnight. "My arm is on fire."

"I know, Mac." Rory touched his hair, then his cheek, and her heart double-tapped when he turned his face into her palm, as if seeking comfort. She tried to pull her hand away but Mac slapped his hand on hers to keep her palm against his cheek. Everyone, even the big, bold

Mac, needed support, a human connection. At the moment she was his.

"It's bad, isn't it?"

What should she say? She didn't want to lie to him, but she had no right to talk to him about his injuries. She shouldn't even be here. "You'll be okay, Mac. No matter what, you'll be okay."

Pain—the deep, dark, emotional kind—jumped into his eyes. His hand moved to her wrist and he pulled her down until her chest rested on his. Her mouth was a quarter inch from his. God, this was so wrong. She shouldn't be doing this. Despite those thoughts ricocheting through her head she couldn't help the impulse to feel those lips under hers, to taste him.

Just once to see if the reality measured up to her imagination.

This would be the perfect time, *the only time*, to find out. She could stop wondering and move the hell past him, past the kiss they'd never shared.

There was no one in the room with them. Nobody would ever know.

His injured state hadn't affected his skills, Rory thought as he took control of the kiss, tipping her head to achieve the precise angle he wanted. His tongue licked its way into her mouth, nipping here, sliding there. Then their tongues met and electricity rocketed through her as she sank into him.

It was all she'd dreamed about. And a lot more.

Rory had no idea how long the kiss lasted. She was yanked back to the present when Mac hissed in pain. Stupid girl! He'd had surgery only hours before! He was in a world of hurt. Mac, she noticed, just lay there, his hand on her thigh and his eyes closed. He was so still. Had he fallen back to sleep? Rory looked down at his big tanned hand and licked her top lip, tasting him there.

It had been just two mouths meeting, tongues dancing, but his kisses could move mountains, part seas, redesign constellations. It had been that powerful. Kissing Mac was an out-of-body experience.

The universe knew what it was doing by keeping them apart. She wasn't looking for a man and she certainly wasn't looking for a man like Mac. Too big, too bold, too confident. A celebrity who had never heard of the word *monogamy*.

He was exactly what she didn't need. Unfaithful. She was perfectly content to fly solo, she reminded herself.

The machine beeped to tell her the program had ended, and Rory started to stand up. The hand squeezing her thigh kept her in place. When she looked at Mac, his eyes were still closed but the corners of his mouth kicked up into a cocky smile.

"Best dream ever," he said before slipping back into sleep.

Two

He'd been dreaming of Rory, something he hadn't done in years, Mac realized as he surfaced out of a pain-saturated sleep. She'd been sitting cross-legged on his bed, her silver-gray eyes dancing. Wide smile, firm breasts, golden-brown hair that was so long, he remembered, that it flirted with her butt…five foot three of petite perfection.

In his dream he'd been French-kissing her and it had felt…man…amazing! Slow, hot, sexy—what a kiss should really be. Okay, he'd had far too many drugs if he was obsessing about a girl he'd wanted to kiss a lifetime ago. Mac shoved his left hand through his hair before pushing himself up using the same hand, trying but failing to ignore the slamming pain in his other arm as he moved.

This was bad. This was very, very bad.

Half lying, half sitting, he closed his eyes and fought the nausea gathering in his throat. Dimly aware of people entering his private hospital room, he fought the pain, pushed down the nausea and concentrated on those silver eyes he'd seen in his dream. The way her soft lips felt under his...

He had been dreaming, right?

"Do you need something for the pain, Mr. McCaskill?"

Mac jerked fully awake and looked into the concerned face of a guy a few years younger than him.

"I'm Troy Hunter, your nurse," he said. "So, some meds? You're due."

"Hell yes," Mac muttered. He usually hated drugs but he slowly rolled onto his good side, presenting his butt to be jabbed as Kade and Quinn walked into the room. "Hey, guys."

Troy glanced at Mac's visitors with his mouth dropped open, looking like any other fan did when the three of them were together...awestruck.

Tall and rock solid, in both stature and personality, Mac wasn't surprised to see Kade and Quinn and so soon after his surgery. They were his friends, his one-time roommates, his colleagues...his family. They were, in every way that counted, his brothers.

After giving him the injection, Troy pulled up Mac's shorts and stood back to look at him, his face and tone utterly professional. "Let's get you sorted out. I need to do my boring nurse stuff and then I'll leave you to talk." He looked more closely at Mac. "You look uncomfortable."

Mac nodded. He was half lying and half sitting but the thought of moving made him break out in a cold sweat. "Yeah, I am."

"I can remedy that." Troy, with surprising ease and

gentleness for a man who was six-three and solid, maneuvered Mac into a position he could live with. While Troy wound a blood pressure cuff around Mac's arm, Kade sat down in the chair on the opposite side of the bed, his expression serious.

"We would appreciate your discretion as to Mac's condition," he told Troy. That voice, not often employed, usually had sponsors, players and random citizens scattering.

Troy, to his credit, didn't look intimidated. "I don't talk about my patients. Ever."

Kade stared at Troy for a long time before nodding once. "Thank you."

They waited in silence until Troy left the room and then Kade turned to him and let out a stream of profanity.

Here it comes, Mac thought, resigned.

"What were you thinking, trying to move that fridge yourself? One call and one of us would've been there to help you!"

Mac shrugged. "It wasn't that heavy. It started to fall and I tried to catch it."

"Why the hell can't you just ask for help?" Quinn demanded. "It's serious, Mac, career-ending serious."

Mac felt the blood in his face drain away. When he could speak, he pushed the words out between dry lips. "That bad, huh?"

Kade looked as white as Mac imagined himself to be. "That bad."

"Physiotherapy?" Mac demanded.

"An outside chance at best," Quinn answered him. He didn't sugarcoat his words, and Mac appreciated it. He needed the truth.

Kade spoke again. "We've found someone to work

with you. She's reputed to be the best at sports rehabilitation injuries."

Neither of his friends met his eyes, and his heart sank to his toes. He knew that look, knew that he wouldn't like what was coming next.

"Who? Nurse Ratched?" he joked.

"Rory Kydd," Kade told him, his face impassive.

"Rory? *What?*" he croaked, not liking the frantic note in his voice. It was bad enough seeing Rory in his dreams but being her patient would mean hitting the seventh level of hell.

There was a reason why he never thought of her, why he'd obliterated that day from his memory. He'd publicly humiliated himself and the world had seen him at his worst. Rory'd had a front-row seat to the behind-the-scenes action.

Saying what he had on that open mic had been bad enough but almost kissing his about-to-be ex's sister was unforgiveable. At the time he'd been thinking of Rory a lot, had been, strangely, attracted to Shay's petite but feisty younger sister. But he should never have caged her in, tempting them both. He knew better than to act on those kinds of feelings, even if his relationship with Shay had been sliding downhill.

His mother's many messy affairs had taught him to keep his own liaisons clean, to remove himself from one situation before jumping into another. He'd forgotten those lessons the moment Rory looked at him with her wide, lust-filled eyes. His big brain shut down as his little brain perked up…

In the months afterward he hadn't missed Shay—too needy, too insecure—but he had missed talking to, teasing, laughing with Rory. She'd been, before he mucked it up, his first real female friend.

That day he'd also unwittingly created a media superstorm and a public persona for himself. He'd been branded a player, a party-hard, commitment-phobic prick whose two objectives in life were to play with a puck and to chase skirts.

They had it half right…

Yes, he liked the occasional party and was commitment-phobic. Yes, he loved to play with a puck and yeah, he had sex, but not as much or with as many woman as was suggested in the tabloids. These days he was a great deal more discriminating about who he took into his bed, and it had been a couple of months since he'd been laid.

He looked down at his arm and scowled. It seemed like it would be a few more.

Quinn gripped the railing at the end of the bed with his massive hands. "Rory is the best and God knows you need the best. We need her because everything we've worked toward for the past five years is about to slip from our fingers because you were too pigheaded to ask for help!"

Kade frowned at their hotheaded friend. "Take it easy, Quinn. It wasn't like he did it on purpose."

No, but it was his fault. Mac tipped his head up to look at the ceiling. He'd failed again today, failed his team, his friends, his future.

And it looked like, once again, Rory would be there to witness it.

There had to be another option. "Find someone else! Anyone else!"

"Don't be a moron!" Quinn told him.

Kade, always the voice of reason, stepped between them before they started to yell. "You'll work with her while we do damage control on our end."

Mac rested his head on his pillow, feeling the sedative effects of whatever the nurse had stuck in him. Ignoring the approaching grogginess, he sucked in some deep breaths and forced his brain to work.

Dammit, why did Vernon Hasselback have to die before they'd concluded the deal they'd all been discussing for the past decade? It was a simple plan: when the time was right he and Kade and Quinn would buy the franchise from Vernon. They'd been working toward this since they were all rookie players and they'd hammered out a detailed plan to raise the cash, which included using their player fees and endorsement money to invest in business opportunities to fund their future purchase of the franchise. The strategy had worked well. Within a decade they had a rock-solid asset base and were, by anyone's standards, ridiculously wealthy. Money wasn't an issue. They could buy the franchise without breaking much of a sweat. But to take the team and its brand to the next level they needed a partner who brought certain skills to the table. Someone who had bigger and better connections in all facets of the media, who could open the doors to mega-sponsorship deals, who had merchandising experience.

Unfortunately, because Vernon died in the bed of his latest mistress, his widow and the beneficiary of his entire estate wasn't inclined to honor his wishes about passing the mantle on to the three of them. Myra wanted to sell the franchise to a Russian billionaire who'd acquired six sports teams in the past two years and was rebranding them to be generic, cardboard cutouts of the teams they once were and mouthpieces for his bland corporation. Kade had convinced Myra to give them some time but they knew she was impulsive and impatient. She would use any setback as an excuse to sell the franchise out from under them, and Mac's injury was a very big setback.

"No one can know how badly I'm injured."

Kade and Quinn nodded. "I'm very aware of that," Kade said. "I also have a potential investor on the hook. He's a loaded Mavericks fan, meets all our requirements and runs a massive media empire so nothing can jeopardize our negotiations. You are one of the reasons he wants to buy the team. He knows you only have a few more years left at this level and he wants you to spend that time mentoring the rookie talent."

So, no additional pressure then. Mac pushed the drowsiness away. "So I have to start playing with his team when the season opens."

"Essentially," Quinn replied, blowing air into his cheeks. "If not sooner."

Mac clenched his jaw in determination. It was the same attitude that had won the team the Stanley Cup two years ago, that had taken him from being just another rookie to one of the most exciting players of his generation. When he decided he was going to do something, achieve something, win something, nothing and nobody got in his way.

"Then I will be on the ice when the season opens."

If that meant working with Rory, so be it. Yes, he'd embarrassed himself a very long time ago. It happened and it was time to move the hell on. He refused to give in or give up—not while there was a chance of getting what he wanted.

"Set up the physio and let's get this party started."

Kade smiled. "You had surgery earlier today. How about getting some sleep first?"

"Are you convinced Rory is the best?" he asked with slightly slurred words.

Kade nodded. "Yeah, she is."

"Get her. Offer her what she needs so she can concentrate on me…" Stupid drugs, Mac thought, making him say the wrong thing. "On my arm. Not me."

Quinn placed a hand on Mac's good shoulder and squeezed. "Go to sleep, bud."

Mac managed a couple more words before slipping off into sleep. "Offer her whatever it takes…"

Rory paused outside the door to Mac's room the next day and hoisted her bag over her shoulder. She pushed her hand through her layered, choppy bob before smoothing out a crease that had appeared in her white and navy tunic, thinking that it had already been a weird day and it wasn't even mid-morning yet. Her day had started with Kade contacting her at the crack of dawn, demanding a meeting to discuss Mac and his injury. She'd told him she could only give Mac her assessment of his injuries and if Mac wanted Kade there, then that was his prerogative. Kade had seemed more amused than annoyed by her crisp tone and had followed up his demands by telling her he had a proposition for her…one that she'd want to hear.

That was intriguing enough to get her to meet with them during her morning break.

Just knock on the door and get this meeting over with, Rory told herself. *You are not nineteen anymore and desperately infatuated with your sister's boyfriend. You're a highly qualified professional who is in high demand. He's a patient like any other.*

Except none of her patients kissed her like he did, or flooded her system with take-me-quick hormones with one look from his navy eyes.

God, you are ridiculous, Rory thought, not amused.

Not allowing herself another minute to hesitate, she briskly knocked on the door, and when she heard his command to enter, she stepped inside. She ignored Mac's two friends standing on either side of his bed and her gaze immediately landed on his face. She told her libido to calm down and gave Mac a *professional* once-over. He was wearing a V-neck T-shirt and someone, probably Troy, had removed the right sleeve. His injured arm was bandaged from wrist to shoulder and was supported by a sling. Clear, annoyed and very wary eyes met hers.

Mac, she also noticed, was in pain but he was fighting his way through it.

Rory looked at his friends, good-looking guys, and smiled. "Hello, Kade. Quinn." Rory stepped toward the bed. "Mac. It's been a while."

Rory held her breath, waiting to see if he remembered the kiss they'd shared, whether he'd say anything about her being in his room the night before. His face remained inscrutable and the look in his eyes didn't change. Thank God, he didn't remember. That would make her life, and this experience, easier.

Or as easy as it could possibly be.

"Rory."

Her name on his lips, she'd never thought she'd hear it again. She desperately wished it wasn't under such circumstances. Rory gathered her wits and asked Quinn to move out of her way. When he did, she stepped up to the bed and pulled the smaller of the two blankets from her bag and placed the control box on the bedside table.

"What are you doing?" Mac demanded. "You're here to talk, not to fuss."

Rory looked him in the eye and didn't react to his growl. "And we will talk, after I set this up."

"What is it?" Kade demanded from his spot on the other side of the bed.

Rory explained how the blanket worked and gently tucked the mat around Mac's injured arm. She started the program, stepped back and folded her arms. "You need some pain meds," she told Mac.

"I'm fine," Mac muttered, his tone suggesting she back off. That wasn't going to happen. The sooner Mac learned that she wasn't easily intimidated, the better. The trick with difficult patients, and obstinate men, was to show no fear.

"You either take some meds or I walk out this door," Rory told him, her voice even. Her words left no doubt that she wasn't bluffing. She picked up the two pills that sat next to a glass of water and waited until Mac opened his hand to receive them. He sent her a dirty look, dry swallowed them and reluctantly chased them down with water from the glass she handed to him.

"You're not a martyr, nor a superhero, so take the meds on schedule," she told him in her best no-nonsense voice. Rory held his hot look and in his eyes she saw frustration morph into something deeper, darker, sexier.

Whoo boy! Internal temperature rising...

"You cut your hair," Mac said, tipping his head to the side.

"Quite a few times in the past decade," Rory replied, her voice tart. One of them had to get this conversation back on track and it looked like she'd been elected.

Fantastic kiss aside, Mac was a potential patient, nothing more, nothing less. She'd be professional if it killed her. She deliberately glanced at her watch and lifted her arched eyebrows. "I have another patient in thirty minutes...so let's skip the small talk and you can tell me why I'm really here."

"I need a physiotherapist."

"Obviously." Rory shrugged. "You're going to need a lot of therapy to get your arm working properly."

"I don't want it to work properly. I want it to be as good as new," Mac stated. "In two months' time."

"In your dreams." Okay, everyone knew Mac was determined but he wasn't stupid. "That's not going to happen. You know that's not possible."

Mac pulled on his stubborn expression. "It *is* going to happen and I'll be back on the ice with or without your help."

Rory sent Kade and Quinn a "help me" look but they just stood there. She was on her own, it seemed. "McCaskill, listen to me. You half ripped a tendon off the bone. It was surgically reattached. We don't know how much damage you've done to the nerves. This injury needs time to heal—"

"I don't have time," Mac told her. "I've got a couple of months and that's it."

Rory shoved her hands into her hair in sheer frustration. "You can sit out another couple of months—you are not indispensable!"

Dammit, her voice was rising. Not good. Do not let him rattle you!

"Two months and I need to be playing. That's it, Rory, that's all the time I've got," Mac insisted. "Now, either I get you to help me do that or I take my chances on someone else."

"Someone you will railroad into allowing you to do what you want, when you want, probably resulting in permanent damage." This was how he'd be in a relationship, she thought. All bossy and stubborn and determined to have his way.

After a lifetime of watching her father steamroll their mother, those weren't characteristics she'd ever tolerate.

"Maybe," was all Mac said.

Rory placed her hands on the bed and leaned forward, brows snapping together. "Why are you doing this, Mac? You have enough money, enough accolades to allow you to sit out a couple of months, a couple of seasons. This is not only unnecessary, it's downright idiotic!"

Mac pulled in a deep breath. For a split second she thought that he might explain, that he'd give her a genuine, responsible reason for his stance. Then his eyes turned inscrutable and she knew it wouldn't happen. "I play. That's what I do."

Rory shook her head, disappointed. He was still the same attention-seeking, hot-dogging, arrogant moron he'd been in his twenties. Did he really believe the hype that he was indispensable and indestructible?

"You're ridiculous, that's what you are," Rory said as she straightened. She sent his friends a blistering look. "You're supporting him in this?"

Kade and Quinn nodded, reluctantly, but they still nodded. Right, so it seemed like she was the only clear thinker in the room. She had to try one more time. "It's one season! You'd probably not even miss the entire season…"

Mac looked resolute. "I have to be there, Rory."

Mac had a will of iron. He was going to play, come hell or high water. She wouldn't be able to change his mind.

"It's my choice and I'll live with the consequences," Mac told her. "I'm not the type to create a storm and then bitch when it rains."

There was no doubting the sincerity in his words. Now, responsibility was something her father had never grasped, she thought. He'd been a serial adulterer and when he got caught—and he *always* got caught—there were a million reasons why it wasn't his fault. And, really, why was she thinking about her father? *Honestly, woman, concentrate!*

She might not agree with what Mac wanted to do, it was a colossal mistake in her professional opinion, but it seemed he was prepared to accept the consequences of his decisions. She had to respect that. But didn't have to be party to his madness.

She dropped her eyes from his face to look at the control box. "There's still twenty minutes to go. I'll ask Troy to disconnect the mat and pack it away. Have a nice life."

Rory turned around and walked toward the door, thinking that her bosses at Craydon's Physiotherapy would throw a hissy fit if they found out she'd turned down the opportunity to treat the great Mac McCaskill.

A part of her wanted to stay, to carry on trying to convince him—them—why this was the stupidest plan in history. *But you're not the jackass whisperer*, her brain informed her.

She had her hand on the door when Mac spoke again. "Rory, dammit…wait!"

Rory turned and saw the silent conversation taking place between the three friends. Kade nodded, Quinn looked frustrated but resigned and Mac looked annoyed.

Well, tough.

"Why can't anything ever be easy with you?" he muttered, and Rory lifted an eyebrow. This from the man who'd dissed Shay on national television and created a public scandal with her sister at the center? Who'd—sort of—made a move on Rory, thereby causing a riff between her and Shay that took many months to heal? Seriously?

"It isn't my job to make things easy for you," Rory retorted. "If there's nothing else…?"

"Hell yes, there's a big something else!" Mac snapped. "And if you repeat it I'll blow a gasket."

Rory just stared at him. The Kydd girls didn't blab. If they did they could've made themselves a nice chunk of change selling their Mac stories to the tabloids.

Mac rubbed the back of his neck with his good hand and proceeded to explain how his being hurt could materially affect the Mavericks. Rory listened, shocked, as Mac dissected the implications of his injury. "If Chenko buys the team, Kade will be replaced as CEO, Quinn's coaching contract won't be renewed and if I'm injured, I'm too old for them to give me another chance. The Mavericks will be turned into another corporate team—and I will *not* let that happen."

Rory took a moment to allow his words to make sense. When they did, her jaw tightened. The Mavericks were a Vancouver institution that had been owned by the Hasselbacks for generations and she knew—thanks to listening to Troy's rants on the subject over the years— that when corporate businesses took over sports teams, the magic dissipated. Traditions were lost; fans were disappointed; the players lost their individuality. It became soulless and clinical. She kept her eyes on Mac, pale-faced and stressed. "And if you do play?"

"Then we have a chance of saving the team."

"How?" Rory demanded.

"It's complicated, and confidential, but we need a particular type of partner, one who has the connections and skills in PR, merchandising, sponsorships. Even though we are retaining control, we are asking for a lot of money for a minor share and we have to accept that I am the face of the team and an essential part of the deal. I have to play." Mac rubbed his forehead with the tips of his fingers, his gesture indicating pain or frustration or exhaustion. Probably all three. "This isn't about me, not this time. Or, at least, it isn't all about me. If I could take the time off I would, I'm not that arrogant. But I need to get back on the ice and, apparently, you're my best bet."

Rory bit her bottom lip, knowing what he was asking was practically impossible. "The chance of you being able to play in two months' time is less than ten percent, Mac. Practically nonexistent."

"I can do it, Rory. You just need to show me how."

She nearly believed him. If anybody could do it then it would be him.

"Mac, you could do yourself some permanent damage."

Mac pressed his lips together. "Again, my choice, my consequences."

God, why did that have to resonate so deeply with her? Okay, so this wasn't *all* about him and his career. A part of it was, of course it was, but she knew how much the Mavericks meant to him. There had been many reports about the bond he shared with his mentor, the now dead owner of the team. The *cheating* dead owner of the Mavericks—dying in his mistress's bed.

Don't think about that, she told herself. With her history of a having a serial cheater for a father, it was a sure way to get her blood pressure spiking.

She had to disregard the emotion around this decision, try to forget he was attempting to save his team, his friends' jobs and the traditions of the Mavericks, which were an essential part of the city's identity. She had to look at his injury, his need and his right to treatment. If this were any other sportsman and not Mac, would she be trying to help him? Yeah, she would.

And really, if she didn't help Mac, Troy might never speak to her again.

She nodded reluctantly. "Okay. I'll help you, as much as I can."

Mac, to her surprise, didn't look jubilant or excited. He just looked relieved and wiped out. "Thank you," he quietly said.

Rory turned to Kade. "You need to contact my office, sign a formal contract with my employers."

Kade grimaced. "Yeah, that's the other thing…we'd like to cut out the middleman."

Rory lifted up her hands in frustration. Was nothing going to be simple today? "What does that mean?"

Kade jerked his head in Mac's direction and Rory saw that his head was back against his pillow and his eyes were closed. "Let's carry on this discussion outside and I'll fill you in."

"Why do I know that you're about to complicate my life even further?" Rory demanded when they were standing in the passage outside Mac's room.

"Because you are, obviously, a very smart woman," Kade said, placing a large hand on her shoulder. "Let's go get some coffee and we'll sort this mess out."

That sounded like an excellent idea since she desperately needed a cup of liquid sanity.

Three

Rory walked into the diner situated around the corner from St. Catherine's Hospital and scanned the tables, looking for her best friend. It had only been an hour since Kade had laid out his terms, and she needed Troy to talk her off the ledge…

Dressed in skinny jeans and a strappy white crop top, she ignored the compliments coming from a table of construction workers on her left. She waved at Troy and smiled at grumbles behind her when they saw her breakfast companion—huge, sexy and, not that they'd ever realize it, gay. With his blond hair, chiseled jaw and hot bod, he had guys—and girls—falling over him and had the social life of a boy band member.

Unlike her who, according to Mr. **Popular**, partied like a nun.

Troy stood up as she approached and she reached up

to place a kiss on his cheek. He'd changed out of his uniform into jeans and a T-shirt but he still looked stressed.

"Rough night? Is Mac being a pain in your backside?" she asked him.

"He's not a problem at all. I was at the home until late. My mom had a bad episode."

Rory sent him a sympathetic look. Troy's mom suffered from dementia and most of his cash went to funding the nursing home he'd put her into. Unfortunately the home wasn't great, but it was the best he could afford.

Rory had decided a long time ago that when she opened her clinic Troy would be her first hire, at a salary that would enable him to move his mom out of that place into a nicer home. Hopefully, if they did well, he could also move out of his horrible apartment and buy a decent car. "Sorry, honey."

Troy shrugged as they sat down on opposite sides of the table. "You look as frazzled as I do. What's up?"

"So much," Rory replied. "Let's order and I'll tell you a story." She pushed the folder she'd been carrying toward Troy. "Look at this."

After they ordered, Rory tapped the file with her index finger. "Read."

"Mark McCaskill?" Troy looked at the label. "Why do you have Open Mac's file?"

Rory pulled a face as the waitress poured them coffee. She'd always loathed that nickname since it was a play on the microphone incident from so long ago, something she didn't need to be constantly reminded of. Then again, his other nickname, PD—short for Panty Dropper—was even worse. "If you're not going to read it then fill me in on all the gossip about him."

Troy frowned. "Why?"

"I'll explain." She waved her hand. "Go. Center and captain of the Vancouver Mavericks hockey team. Incredible player, one of the very best. Dates a variety of women. What else?"

Troy rested his forearms on the table, his face pensive. "Well, he's spokesperson for various campaigns, epilepsy being one of them. He sits on the boards of a few charities, mostly relating to children. He's also, thanks to investing in bars, restaurants and food trucks, one of the wealthiest bachelors in town. He's also supremely *haawwwt*," Troy added. "And surprisingly nice, even though I know how stressed he must be wondering if this injury will keep him out for the season."

Mac—nice? Yeah, sure.

Troy flicked the file open and flipped through the pile of papers. "You're treating him?"

Rory nodded and Troy looked confused. "But this isn't a Craydon file," he added, referring to the distinctive yellow-and-blue patient files used at the physiotherapy practice she worked for. "What gives, Rorks?"

Rory folded her arms across her chest and tapped her foot, her big, silver-gray eyes tight with worry. How much to tell him? As much as she could, she decided, he was her best friend. She trusted him implicitly and valued his judgment. Still, sharing didn't come easily to her so she took a moment to work out what to say. "Mac and I have a…history."

Troy's snort was disbelieving. "Honey, you're not his type. He dates tall, stacked, exotic gazelles."

Rory scowled. She knew what type of woman Mac dated. She saw them every time she opened a newspaper or magazine. "I know that I am short, and flat-chested," Rory snapped. "You don't need to rub it in."

"I didn't mean it like that," Troy quietly stated. "Yeah, you're short but you have a great figure, you know that you do. And there's nothing wrong with your chest."

"Like you'd know," Rory muttered.

"I know that you desperately need some masculine hands on your boobs and on other more exciting parts of your body. It's been a year, eighteen months, since you've had some action?"

Actually it was closer to two years, but she'd rather die than admit that to Mr. Cool. "Can we concentrate on my McCaskill problem please?"

"He's a problem?"

"You've forgotten that Shay was dating him during the open-mic disaster."

Troy's mouth dropped open. "I *did* forget that. He said he was bored with her, that monogamy was for the birds."

"Yep. Obviously that's a position he still holds."

Troy leaned back so the waitress could put their food down. He frowned at Rory's sarcastic comment. "Honey, that was a long time ago and he was young. Shay's moved on…what's the problem?"

"He's a man-slut. It annoys me."

"It shouldn't. He didn't cheat on *you*," Troy pointed out, and Rory stared down at her plate.

No, he'd almost cheated on her sister with her. The intention had been there. He would've cheated if Rory hadn't stopped him. He was just like her father and exactly the last person in the world she should be attracted to.

It made absolutely no sense at all.

She'd never told Troy—or anyone—what had happened between her and Mac and she still couldn't. Hurting her sister hadn't been her finest moment.

"Okay, admittedly, Mac is not the poster boy for love and commitment so I kind of get your antipathy to him since you have such a huge issue with infidelity," Troy said after taking a sip of his coffee.

"Doesn't everyone?" Rory demanded. "Have issues with it?"

"No. And if they do, they don't take it to the nth degree like you do. Hell, Rorks, I recall you not accepting a date from a perfectly nice guy because you said he had a 'cheating face.'"

Rory ignored his air quotes and lifted her nose in the air. "Okay, maybe that was wrong of me."

"Wrong of you? It was properly ridiculous."

Troy tapped the folder before he attacked his eggs. "Tell me how this came about."

Rory filled him in and Troy listened, fascinated.

"So, they want you, widely regarded as the best sports rehab physio in the area, to work on Mac. Why didn't they just approach the clinic directly and hire you that way?"

She'd asked Kade the same question. "They are going to keep the extent of Mac's injury a secret from the public and the fans. They'll admit that he's pulled a muscle or something minor but they don't want it getting out that his injury is as bad as it is."

"Why the secrecy?"

"Sorry, I can't tell you that." Troy, to his credit, didn't push. "Kade asked me to take a leave of absence from the clinic to treat Mac."

Troy's eyebrows lifted. "Seriously?"

"Yeah."

"And you said yes, no, hell, no?"

"Thanks to the fact that I am a workaholic, I have

nearly two and a half months of vacation due to me that I have to either use or lose."

Troy just looked at her, waiting for her to continue.

"Kade offered me twenty grand for six weeks and another thirty if I get Mac back into condition by the time the season starts in two months."

"Fifty K?" Troy's mouth fell open. After a moment of amazed silence he spoke again. "With that sort of money you could open your own practice like you've been dreaming of doing."

And, more important, she could employ him. Rory nodded. "Yeah. I want to set up a clinic that isn't a conveyor belt of only treating the patient's pain—"

"No need to go on, I've been listening to you ramble on about your clinic for years." Troy's smile was full of love. "And Kade's offer will allow you to establish this clinic without having to take a loan or use the money you were saving for a house."

"Essentially."

"It sounds like a no-brainer, Rorks," Troy said quietly.

Rory sucked her bottom lip between her teeth. It did, didn't it? "Except for two rather major points."

"Which are?"

"First, I am stupidly, crazily attracted to Mac. Nobody makes my blood move like he does." She glared at Troy. "Don't you dare laugh! How am I supposed to treat him when all I want to do is crawl all over him?"

Troy hooted, vastly amused.

"Second, and more important, I don't think I can fix him, Troy, and especially not in two months." Troy stopped laughing and stared at her.

"I don't think he's got a hope in hell."

"Except that you are forgetting one thing…" Troy

cocked his head at her and slowly smiled. "When Mac McCaskill decides he wants something, he'll move hell and high water to get it. Everyone knows that if Mac says he is going to do something, he'll get it done. He doesn't know what *failure* means."

Yet he'd failed Shay and, in a roundabout way, failed her. He wasn't anywhere as perfect as Troy thought him to be.

The next morning Rory knocked on Mac's door and stuck her head inside after he told her to come in.

"I'm in the bathroom, I'll be with you in a sec," Mac called, so Rory sat down in the visitors' chair, her bag at her feet. Inside the folder that she placed on her knees was a signed contract to be Mac's physiotherapist for the next two months.

A little over two months…nine or so weeks. Rory felt panic bubble in her throat and she rubbed her hands over her face. She wasn't sure if she was scared, excited or horrified. A clinic, the last piece of a down payment for a house, a job for Troy, she reminded herself.

If she continued to save as she'd been doing, it would take another two years to gather what they were prepared to pay her in two months. This was a once-in-a-lifetime deal and she would be a moron to turn to it down. As she'd explained to Troy, there was just one little problem—she had to work with Mac, around Mac, *on* Mac. The chemistry between them hadn't changed. She was as attracted to him as she had been at nineteen, possibly even more. Young Mac had been charismatic and sexy and charming but Mac-ten-years-on was a potent mix of power, strength and determination that turned her to jelly. Kade might be the Mavericks' CEO, and Quinn was no pushover, but yesterday in this same room, Mac, despite his pain, was their undisputed leader. He had, thanks to his mental strength, pushed through pain and taken charge of the meeting.

Mac was determined and had a will to win that was second to none. He was also a rule breaker and a risk taker and utterly bullheaded.

Exactly the type of man she always avoided. They were fun and interesting and compelling, but they broke hearts left, right and center. Sometimes, as was the case with her father, they broke the same hearts over and over again.

She was too smart to let that happen to her.

Mac hated to take orders, but if she had any hope of fixing his arm, then he had to listen to her, do as she said when she said it. That would be a challenge. Mac, alpha male, was overly confident about his own abilities. She'd seen him in action; if he wanted to run a six-minute mile, he did it. If he wanted to improve the speed on his slap shot, he spent hours and hours on the ice until he was satisfied. If Mac wanted to fix his arm, he would work on it relentlessly. Except that muscles and injuries needed time to heal and, especially since his injury was so serious, he had to be careful. If he pushed the recovery process he could suffer irreversible damage and his career would be over. Permanently.

Yet if he wasn't healed in two months, the Mavericks, as Vancouver knew them, would be gone, and while she might have a brand-new shiny clinic, she might not have any clients if she couldn't fix the great Mac McCaskill.

Rock, meet hard place.

"Rory."

Rory snapped her head up to see Mac standing in the

doorway of the bathroom, wearing nothing more than a pair of designer denims and a deep scowl. His hair was wet and he'd wrapped a plastic bag around his arm to keep it dry. He hadn't managed the buttons on his jeans and through the open flaps she could see the white fabric of his, thank goodness, underwear. His chest was damp and a continent wide, lightly covered in brown hair in a perfect *T* that tapered into a fine trail of hair that crossed those fabulous washboard abs.

Sexy, almost-naked man in open blue jeans, Rory thought... *I could so jump you right now.*

Mac tried to button his jeans with one hand and swore creatively. Very creatively, Rory thought. She'd never before heard that combination of words strung together.

"Sorry," Mac muttered when he lifted aggravated eyes to meet hers. "But I am so damn frustrated I could punch something."

Rory placed the folder on the table next to her and slowly stood up. "Want some help?"

Mac looked at his watch and then scowled in the direction of the door. He looked as uncomfortable as she felt.

"Kade was supposed to come and help me get dressed and drive me home..."

"You've been discharged?"

"Yeah. The more time I spend here, the better the chances are of the press finding me." Mac lifted a muscled, tanned shoulder. "Besides, it's just my arm, the rest of me works just fine."

And looks pretty good too. Okay, get a grip, Kydd. You're a professional, remember? Try to act like one.

She rocked on her heels. "So, do you want some help?"

Mac looked at the door again and released a heavy sigh. "Yeah. Please."

Rory tried to keep her face blank as she reached for the flaps of his jeans. *Just get it done, fast*, she told herself, so she grabbed the first button and slotted it through its corresponding hole, brushing something that felt very masculine in the process, and not as soft as it should be. Keeping her head down, she moved on to button number two and repeated the action, very conscious of the growing bulge beneath her hands. She was flushed by the time she slotted in the last button, and she stepped back and pushed her hair out of her eyes.

She would not acknowledge his halfway-there erection. It was a conditioned response and something he couldn't help. Her hands were fiddling around his crotch; she could've been three hundred pounds with a mustache and he would've been turned on. It wasn't personal.

But damn, he was impressive… *Ignore, ignore, ignore.*

"Whoever packed for you was an idiot. Elasticized track pants or shorts would've been a better option," she stated, feeling hot from the inside out.

Mac ignored her comment and reached out to hold a strand of her hair. "I loved your long hair but this style works for you too."

"Uh…" Her brain needed oxygen. She couldn't think when he was so close, when she could smell the soap on his skin, could count every individual eyelash, see the different shades of dark blue in his eyes. What had he said? Something about her hair…

"Thanks."

Mac pushed her hair behind her ear and his fingers brushed her skin, and Rory couldn't help but shiver. This wasn't good, she thought, taking a huge step backward. He was dangerous, working with him was dangerous…

she shouldn't do this. It was a train wreck waiting to happen.

Clinic, house, practice, dream, her brain reminded her.

Shay, Mac cheating, men are inherently faithless, her soul argued. *Attraction leads to love and love leads to betrayal. Not happening.*

Rory jammed her hands into the back pockets of her jeans and nodded at Mac's bare feet. "Shoes?"

"Flip-flops," Mac replied, walking over to the bed and picking up a royal blue, V-necked T-shirt. He pulled the opening over his head and managed to slide his un-injured arm through the corresponding opening. Then he looked at his injured, immobile arm and cursed again.

"There's an art to dressing yourself when you're injured," she told him. Idiot that she was, she got up close and personal with him again, but this time she tried to avoid touching him as she pulled the shirt up and over his head. Shaking it out, she found the sleeve to his injured arm and gently slid the shirt up and over so that it bunched around his shoulder. He ducked his head through the opening, shoved his other arm through and the fabric fell down his chest.

It was wrong to hide such a work of art, Rory thought. "Thanks."

Rory looked up at him, her head barely scraping his shoulder. God, he was big, six foot three of solid, sexy man. "Anything else?"

Mac shook his head. "No. I'm okay." He sat down on the edge of the bed and gestured to the chair she'd been sitting on earlier. "Take a seat, we need to talk."

Rory wasn't under any illusion that his quietly stated words were anything other than an order. Her spine straightened and her mouth tightened. Since there were, actually, a few things she had to say to him, she sat down and crossed her legs.

"You've had a little time to read over my chart, to assess the damage." Mac stretched out his long legs and sent her a hard look. "Thoughts?"

Rory pulled in a breath. "I presume you don't want me to sugarcoat it for you?"

"Hell, no."

Okay, then. "You ripped the lateral ulnar collateral ligament, luckily not completely from the bone, and it was surgically repaired. You also sprained the radial collateral ligament and the annular ligament."

"Which means?" Mac demanded, impatient.

"You're in a lot of pain and the injuries won't be easy to fix."

Mac's expression hardened. "Oh, they will be fixed. How much time does it normally take?"

She hated these types of questions; there were too many variables. Like bruised, broken and battered hearts, there was no time frame for recovery. "C'mon, Mac, you know better than to ask me that! Some people heal quicker, some never do. I can't answer that!"

"Can it be done in two months?" Mac pushed for an answer.

Rory tipped her head back to look at the ceiling. "I think you are asking for a miracle."

"Miracles happen," Mac calmly stated. "What can I do to jump-start the healing process?"

Rory thought for a minute. "My electromagnetic mat, for a start. We'll do treatments three or four times a day. It's noninvasive and will get the blood moving through the damaged capillaries. Anti-inflammatory drugs to take the swelling down.

"When *I* think it's time, we will start doing exercises," Rory added, and as she expected Mac's scowl deepened.

"I'm a professional player, I can take the pain," Mac said through gritted teeth. He wasn't listening to her, Rory realized. Did men like him ever listen to what they didn't want to hear?

"It's not about what you can endure, McCaskill!" Rory snapped. "It's about not making a very bad injury ten times worse! You will start exercising that arm when I say you can, with the exercises I approve, and not a minute before."

Mac glared at her and she kept her face impassive. "I'm not joking, Mac, this point is not up for negotiation."

Mac rubbed the back of his neck with his free hand. "Look, Rory, I'm not trying to be a jerk but a lot is riding on me being able to play in nine or so weeks."

"I understand that, but what you don't understand is that if you push, you might never play ever again! Is that a risk you are prepared to take?"

For a moment, Mac looked desolate, then his inscrutable expression fell back into place. He didn't respond to her question but she knew she'd made her point. "I don't want you to pussyfoot around me. You push me and you push me hard. As soon as you can."

He didn't allow for weakness, Rory thought, his body had to function how he wanted it to. She suspected he carried that trait into his relationships. His way or the highway...

Reason number fifty-four why they would never have managed to make a relationship work.

Going back to their actual conversation and pushing aside the craziness in her head, Rory realized that was the only concession he was prepared to make and she mentally declared their argument a draw. Good enough for her. She stood up to leave and gestured to the folder on the table. "I've signed your contract and I've been released from my job for ten weeks. We need to set up a schedule for when it's convenient for me to see you. To check on your mobility, to wrap your arm in the mat."

Mac shifted on the bed. "Where do you live?"

"I have an apartment in Eastside."

"I live in Kitsilano, not far from here actually. Commuting to my place three or four times a day is unnecessary. I have a spare room. You should move in."

Yeah, no way. Ever. That was far more temptation than she could handle. She needed to keep as much distance between them as she possibly could and if that meant trekking across town daily, or three or four times a day, then that was what she would do. She and Mac together in a house, alone, was asking for trouble. Trouble she needed like a hole in her heart.

Rory slowly shook her head.

"C'mon, Rory, it's not a big deal." Mac was obviously used to women moving in to his house on a regular basis but she wasn't going to follow those lemmings off a cliff. Nope, she'd deal with the devil if it meant the chance to run her own clinic, to treat her patients the way she wanted to, but she'd keep this particular devil at a safe distance.

"I'll live with the driving." She pulled her cell from her back pocket. "What's your address?"

Mac told her and also gave her his cell number, handing his phone to her so she could input hers into his state-of-the-art phone. When they were done, Rory looked at the door. She should leave. She picked up her bag and pulled it over her shoulder. "I'll see you later this evening. Around five?"

Mac nodded. She was almost at the door when Mac spoke again. "Are we not going to discuss it? At all? Pretend it didn't exist?"

Rory turned around slowly and lifted her hands. "What's the point? You insulted her on national television, we almost kissed, my sister heard us talking. She had to deal with a broken heart while she was stalked and hassled by the press. And she didn't talk to me for months."

Mac's jaw tightened and his lips thinned. "I'm sorry, I didn't think of that."

"You weren't thinking at all that day," Rory told him, her voice tart. "Admittedly, I wasn't either." Rory exhaled. "Look, it happened a long time ago and there's nothing to talk about."

Mac released a laugh that was heavy with derision and light on joy. "You're right. Nothing…except that the chemistry hasn't gone away. We're still attracted to each other."

She wished she could deny it but that would be a bald-faced lie, and she suspected Mac could still read her like a book. "I don't sleep with my patients."

Mac didn't look convinced. "You think we can resist each other? We'll be spending an enormous amount of time together and biology is biology."

"Unlike you, I can control myself," Rory told him primly.

Mac lifted an arrogant eyebrow. "Really? You think chemistry like ours just evaporates?" Mac snorted. "So if I kiss you, right here, right now…you can resist me?"

Rory rolled her eyes. "I know you find this hard to believe but there are women who can."

Mac smiled slowly. "You're not one of them."

Unfortunately he was probably right. Not that Rory would allow him to put his theory to the test. He'd already kissed her once and, despite the fact that he'd been as high as a kite, the kiss had blown her boots off. There was no way she would confirm his suspicions.

"Get over yourself, McCaskill. You're confusing me with those pretty, brainless bunnies that drop in and out of your life."

Mac took a step closer and his hurt arm brushed her chest. "Jealous?"

She wasn't even going to ask herself that question, mostly because she wasn't a hundred percent convinced that she wasn't jealous. Rory made an effort to look condescending. For good measure, she patted his cheek. "Bless your delusional little heart."

Mac's eyes darkened with fury, or lust, who knew, and he wrapped his good arm around her waist and pulled her up onto her toes, slamming his mouth against hers. No drugs affected his performance this time. This was Mac, pure and undiluted.

He didn't tease or tangle. The kiss was hard, demanding, harsh and urgent. *Hot.* On his lips she could taste her own bubblegum-flavored lip balm mixed with his toothpaste and the stringent tang of the mouthwash he must've used earlier. Rory felt his hand drop down her back to palm her butt, kneading her cheek until she was squirming, trying to get closer, needing to climb inside his mouth, his skin, to feel wrapped up within his heat…

Mac jerked back. "Dammithell." These words were followed by a string of others and it took Rory a minute to realize that his pale face and harsh breathing wasn't a result of the kiss, but from her bumping his injured arm.

She winced and lifted her hands to do something to help. When he took another step back she realized she'd done more than enough. Of everything.

Rory watched as Mac slowly straightened, as his breathing evened out. When she was sure he wasn't about to fall over, she slapped her hands on her hips. "That's not happening again. Ever."

One corner of Mac's mouth lifted to pull his lips up into a cocky smile. "Of course it won't," he replied, his voice oozing sarcasm. "Because we have no chemistry and you can resist me."

Lord give me patience. Rory yanked the door open and barreled into the passageway. *Because if You give me strength I'm going to need bail money, as well.*

Four

She'd had her hand on his crotch.

His life was currently a trash fire—messy and ugly—and all he could think about was how Rory's fingers felt brushing across his junk, how much he wanted her hand encircling his erection, how nobody had ever managed to set his blood on fire like that pint-size fairy who needed her attitude adjusted.

Mac glared at the half-open door, dropped into the chair and leaned his head back against the wall. He was not having a good day; it was just another day from hell in a series of hellish days in Hell City. He hadn't felt this crazy since that disaster ten years ago.

Wah, wah, wah... Admittedly, he sounded like a whiny ten-year-old, but wasn't he allowed to? Just this once? He hadn't been this unsure of his future since he'd hitched a ride out of his hometown fifteen years ago. And even then, he hadn't been that worried. He'd made excellent grades in school and a rare talent on the ice had translated into a full scholarship to college. He'd then been recruited to play for the Mavericks and earned serious money. By investing in companies and start-ups, he'd earned more. Considerably more. He was, by anyone's definition, a success. He was living the life, incredibly wealthy, popular, successful.

Despite his rocky upbringing, he believed he was, mostly, a functioning adult, fully committed to steering his own ship. He had an active social life; he genuinely liked women, and while he didn't "do" commitment, he wasn't the player everyone assumed him to be. Sure, he'd dated one or two crackpots but he'd managed to remain friends with most of the women he'd dated.

So, if he was a successful adult, why was he so insanely pissed off right now? Bad things happened to good people all the time...

He'd be handling this better if his fight with the fridge had only impacted his own life, his own career. Like that long ago incident with Shay, his actions had not only hurt himself but could hurt people he cared about too. He knew what it felt like to be collateral damage. He'd been the collateral damage of his mother's bad choices and perpetual negativity.

To this day, he could still hear her lack of enthusiasm for anything he said or did. His mother was the reason he had no intention of settling down. In his head commitment equaled approval and he'd be damned if he ever sought approval from a woman again. He didn't want it and he didn't need it...

Wanting approval was like waiting to catch a boat at an airport. Constantly hopeless. Endlessly disappointing.

It was far easier not to give people, a woman, the opportunity to disappoint him. Rory—funny, loyal, interesting—was a problem. He didn't care for the fact that he *liked* her, that this blast from his past excited him more than he thought possible.

You are overthinking this, idiot. This is just about sex, about lust, about attraction.

It had to be because he wouldn't allow it to be anything else.

That being said, he was playing with fire in more ways than one. Yes, Rory might be the best physiotherapist around and eminently qualified to treat him, but she was also his famous ex's sister. If the press found out about this new connection, they would salivate over the story. If they then found out he and Rory were attracted to each other they'd think they'd died and gone to press heaven.

There were many reasons to downplay his injury, but the thought of putting Rory through the same hell Shay experienced at the hands of those rabid wolves made him feel sick. *Not happening*, he decided.

Not again.

Thank God she'd refused his asinine suggestion to move in with him. Wasn't that a perfect example of how his brain shut down whenever she was around? If she moved in he'd give them, mmm, maybe five minutes before they were naked and panting.

He had no choice but to keep his attraction to her under control, keep his distance—emotionally and physically. He had to protect himself and protect her, and the only way to do both was to put her in the neutral zone—that mental zone he'd created for people, events, stuff that didn't, or shouldn't, impact him.

So he'd put her there, but he wasn't convinced, in any way, shape or form, that she'd actually remain there.

Rory stood on the pavement outside Mac's Kitsilano home, the key Mac had given her earlier in her hand. The house wasn't what she'd expected. She'd thought he'd have a blocky, masculine home with lots of concrete and steel. She hadn't expected the three-story with its A-pitched roof, painted the color of cool mist with dark gray accents. It looked more like a home and less like the den of sin she'd expected.

Rory walked up the steps to the front door, slid the key into the lock and entered the house, stopping to shove the key back into the front pocket of her jeans. There was good art on the wall, she noticed as she moved farther into the living area, and the leather furniture was oversize and of high quality. A massive flat-screen TV dominated one wall, and apart from a couple of photographs of the three Maverick-teers, there wasn't anything personal in the room. Mac had no hockey memorabilia on display, nothing to suggest he was the hottest property on ice. She'd expected his walls to be covered with framed jerseys and big self-portraits. Instead his taste ran to original art and black-and-white photographs.

"Rory?" Mac's voice drifted down the stairs. "Come on up. Top floor."

She walked back into the hallway and up the stairs. She reached the second floor, looked down the passage and wished she could explore. Instead she jogged up the short, second flight that ended at the entrance to an expansive bedroom. The high pitch of the roof formed the paneled ceiling. The room was dominated by a massive king-size messy but empty bed. Rory looked around and saw Mac sprawled on a long sofa on the far side of the room. His head rested against the arm and his eyes were closed. Pain had etched deep grooves next to his mouth. His normally tanned skin was pale and he was taking long, slow, measured breaths.

His eyes didn't open but his mouth did. "Hey, were there any press people outside when you let yourself in?"

"No, why?"

"Just asking."

Rory dropped her gaze and her eyebrows lifted at his unbuttoned white shirt, his unzipped gray suit pants and his bare feet. An aqua tie lay on the seat next to him, on top of what was obviously a matching suit jacket. Black shoes and socks sat on the wood coffee table in front of him.

Oh, hell, no! "Going somewhere?"

"Planning on it."

"The only place you are going is back to bed." Rory folded her arms against her chest. "You need a full-time nurse, McCaskill."

If she moved in then she could stop him from making stupid decisions. But would she be able to stop *herself* from making stupid decisions, like sleeping with him?

"I don't need a nurse, I need a morphine drip," Mac responded, finally opening his eyes and squinting at her.

"Would you care to explain why you are all dressed up when you should be in bed, resting that injury?" Rory demanded, annoyed. This was what she'd been worried about. Mac thought that he was a superhero, that the usual consequences of surgery and injury didn't apply to him.

Despite the fact that he was a very intelligent man, the wheel was turning but the hamster seemed to be dead.

"Don't give me grief, Rory," Mac said, sounding exhausted. "Trust me, there is no place I'd rather be than in bed but something came up."

"A wine auction? A ball? A poker game?" Rory asked, her eyebrows lifting. Mac was very active on the Vancouver social scene and he was, with the women who spun in and out of his life, invited to all the social events.

Mac, despite his pain, managed to send her an annoyed glance. "Myra Hasselback, current owner of the Mavericks, is holding an end-of-season cocktail party for the sponsors, management and staff. I can't miss it. As Captain, I am expected to be there."

"But…" Rory looked from him to his arm and back again. "Does she know that you are hurt?"

Mac's smile was grim. "Oh, she knows, but she doesn't know how bad it is. Kade told her it's a slight sprain, nothing for her to worry about. She told Kade to tell me she was looking forward to seeing me tonight. Besides, she knows I would move heaven and earth to be at the cocktail party. It's a tradition that was important to Vernon." Mac sat up slowly. "She'd suspect something if I wasn't there."

"Judging by your pale face and pain-filled eyes she's going to suspect something anyway." Rory sighed her frustration. "What do the other two Maverick-teers have to say on the subject?"

"They wanted me to fake a stomach bug or an allergic reaction to medication."

"Not a bad idea. Why not go with that?"

Mac looked uncomfortable. "I suppose I could but I don't want to give her an excuse to arrive on my doorstep after the party is over to check on me."

"She's done that before?" Rory asked.

Mac looked uncomfortable, and not from the pain. "Yeah, once or twice."

Rory turned his words over, recalling the thirty-year difference between Myra and her dead husband. Ah, the widow wanted naked comforting.

Rory wanted to ask if he'd slept with Myra but she mentally slapped her hand across her mouth. She had no right to ask that but... *But* nothing. She had no right to know.

"Anyway, about the party, I need to be there. The speculation will be endless if I don't attend. It would raise a lot of questions, questions I do not want to answer." Mac looked stubborn. "No, it's better for me to act like everything is normal as far as I possibly can. So, will you please help me finish getting dressed?"

"I'm not happy about this, Mac."

"I know. I'm not either."

But he'd go, Rory realized. He needed rest and time for that injury to heal but he would do what he always did. If this was his intended pace, they were in for some serious problems.

Rory walked across his bedroom to stand in front of the huge windows and watched a container ship navigate the sound. But her thoughts weren't on the gorgeous view, they were on that stubborn man who didn't know the meaning of the words *slow down, take it easy*. To heal, Mac needed rest and lots of it. It was that simple, that imperative.

That difficult.

Dammit, she was going to *have* to move in here. His arm, his career, the Mavericks were at risk and she was balking because he had the ability to melt the elastic on her panties. She was better, stronger, a great deal more professional than that.

She was a smart, independent, focused woman who could say no to what wasn't good for her. Who could, who *would*, keep their relationship strictly professional.

"Don't even think about it. You are not now, or ever, going to move in."

Dammit! Had he started reading her mind now? When? How? "But you suggested it earlier."

"I changed my mind. It would be a terrible idea. Moving on, are you going to help me or not?" Mac demanded, sounding irritable.

She wanted to be petty and tell him to go to hell but she knew he was stubborn enough to dress himself. *One fight at a time*, Rory thought.

"Yes. If you take some painkillers," Rory stated, her tone discouraging any arguments. "You look like a breath of wind could blow you over, Mac, and there is no way anyone will believe you have a slight sprain if you walk into that room looking like that. Painkillers...that's my demand."

"They make me feel like hell. Spacey and out of control," Mac muttered.

"I have some in my bag. They aren't as strong as yours but they'll take the edge off." Rory looked at her watch. "What time do you need to leave for this party?"

"Kade and Quinn should be here any moment." A door slammed below them and the corner of Mac's mouth kicked up. "Speaking of the devil and his sidekick..."

"Who is the devil and who is the sidekick?" Rory asked.

"Depends on the occasion. We all have our moments."

Now *that* she could believe. Rory jammed her hands

into the pockets of her jeans and rocked on her heels. "I'll run downstairs to get those painkillers and one of your sidekicks can come back up and help you dress."

"Aw, they aren't as pretty as you. Nor do they smell as good."

"I'm not so sure…they are both very pretty and they do smell good," she teased.

Mac sent her a narrow-eyed look. "Do not flirt with my friends."

He sounded jealous. But that was probably just her imagination running off again.

"Why on earth not?" Rory asked, deliberately ignoring the heat building between her legs and the thump-thump of her heartbeat.

"I wouldn't like it," Mac growled.

Rory forced herself to do a massive eye roll as she edged her way to the door. "I think you are confusing me with someone who might actually give a damn."

"Rory?"

When she turned, Mac did a slow perusal of her body. She felt like he'd plugged her into the electricity grid. "Seriously, no flirting."

"Seriously, you're an idiot." Rory made a big production of her sigh. "They really should invent a vaccine to prevent that."

The next morning Mac, dressed in a T-shirt and a pair of sweatpants, walked into his kitchen and, ignoring his two friends sitting at his table, headed straight for the coffeepot. Filling a cup to the brim, he gulped a sip, shuddered, swallowed another mouthful and prayed the caffeine would hit his system in the next thirty seconds. He felt like death warmed over. His arm was on fire, his head was pounding and he wanted to climb back into bed and sleep for a week. He supposed being out last night and pretending he was fine contributed to his less than stellar mood.

As did the drugs and the anesthetic, he realized. It always took time for drugs to work their way out of his system. He felt like a wet blanket was draped over his head. He'd work through it, as he always did.

He jerked his head at his friends and looked around the kitchen. "Where's Rory?"

"She went home," Quinn replied, taking a donut from the box on the table and biting into it.

"But…" Mac frowned, looking toward the front door. "I thought she was here earlier. She wrapped that mat thing around my arm."

"She was. Now she's gone," Quinn replied, stretching out his long legs. "Need anything? I can make eggs."

Mac shook his head, smiling internally. Quinn, their resident badass, was a nurturer at heart, intent on making the world around him better and brighter for the people he loved. There weren't many people he showed his softer side to. To the world he was an adrenaline-addicted bad boy, speed-freak player, but his family and close friends knew he would move heaven and earth for the people he loved.

"I'm good, thanks."

Kade pushed back his chair and pulled back the cuff of his shirt to look at his watch. It was new, Mac realized, and damn expensive. "I've got to get moving, my morning is crazy."

"Can you give me fifteen minutes?" Mac asked, picking up his coffee. "We need to talk."

He didn't want to do this. Frankly he was considering abdicating all his rights to adulthood at this point and going back to bed, but he leaned against the counter and held his cup in his good hand.

"What's up?" Quinn asked.

"This situation is a classic cluster…" Mac allowed his words to trail away and rubbed the back of his neck. He needed air. This kitchen was far too small for three six-foot-plus men.

"Let's go outside." Mac placed his cup on the table and grabbed a donut. Maybe a sugar rush would make him feel better. He took one bite, grimaced and tossed the donut back into the box.

Kade and Quinn exchanged a long, worried look, which made Mac grind his back teeth. He was about to knock some heads together—okay, he couldn't beat up a worm at the moment but the thought was there—when Kade stood up and walked over to the open doors that led to the small patio. Mac followed him out into the sunshine and Quinn lumbered to his feet to do the same.

They looked over the houses below them, across False Creek and toward the Lions Gate Bridge and the mountains beyond. God, he loved this city and its endless, changing views. He couldn't think of living anywhere else; this was home. He'd had offers from teams all over the continent but he'd never been willing to be traded, and Vernon had kept him, and Kade and Quinn. Unless they managed to buy the Mavericks, that would all change. Mac didn't mind change, as long it was the change *he* wanted.

"I'm really worried about the press finding out about my injury," Mac quietly stated.

Kade rested his forearms on the railing and cocked his head to look at Mac. "We put out a press release stating you have a minor injury and that you should be fine soon."

Not good enough, Mac decided. "There's too much at stake."

Quinn frowned. "But only the three of us and Rory know the truth. The doctors and nurses are bound by patient confidentiality. I think we'll be okay."

Mac rubbed his chin. "Until the press realizes I am spending an enormous amount of time with my ex-girlfriend's sister."

It took a minute for the implications of that scenario to register with his friends. When it did, they both looked uneasy. Kade rubbed his chin. "That was the incident that started their obsession with what we do, who we date."

Mac felt a spurt of guilt. "Yeah. And if they find out about Rory, how will we explain why we are spending time together?" He frowned. "I will not tell them we are seeing each other, in any capacity. God, that would open up a nasty can of worms, not only for Rory but for Shay, as well."

"And even if you told them she was your physio, that statement would raise questions as to why we aren't using our resident physios, why we need her to treat you," Kade said. "Especially since your injury is supposed to be a minor one."

"Bingo."

Quinn swore. "What's that saying about lies and tangles we weave?"

"Shut up, Shakespeare." Kade stood up, looking worried. So was Mac. He'd spent most of the night thinking about how they could avoid this very wide, imminent pitfall.

Quinn leaned his hip against the railing and narrowed

his eyes. "We've painted ourselves into a corner. We've downplayed your injury and said you'll be fine in a couple of weeks. When you are not fine in a week or two, how are we going to explain that?"

"I have a solution," Mac said. "I don't like it—in fact, I hate it. I need to be here, working with you on the deal to purchase the team. But it's all I can think of…"

"Well?" Quinn demanded, impatient.

"I need to get out of the city."

Kade tapped his finger against his chin. "Yeah, but any fool can see you are more badly injured than we say you are. We got away with lying once, only because the injury was brand-new, but we can't keep shoveling that story. Your eyes are dull, you can tell you are on hectic painkillers."

"I'll stop the drugs," Mac insisted.

"Now who is being stupid?" Quinn demanded.

"Last night you hadn't taken the proper pain meds and you looked like a walking corpse," Kade said. "The point is that people will notice and that will lead to complications. I think your instinct is right. It's best for you to leave. We can tell Myra, the press, anyone who cares that you are taking an extended vacation."

Mac swore. "I have no idea where to go. There's nowhere I *want* to go."

"The chalet in Vail?" Quinn suggested.

"No snow, and even if there was, I couldn't ski. Torture."

"An African safari?"

"Done that." God, didn't he sound like a spoiled brat?

"What about the Cap de Mar property?" Kade persisted.

He'd already considered Puerto Rico and he'd immediately dismissed that idea. Too hot, too isolated, too sexy…

"Are you nuts?" Mac rolled his eyes.

"No," Kade replied, his voice calm as he ticked off points on his fingers. "Not big on ice hockey so you'll be able to fly under the radar. Two, there's sun, sea and beaches…where's the problem? Three, you love it there. Four, Rory will go with you and she'll do her treatment there."

A vision of Rory dressed in nothing more than four triangles flipped onto the big screen of his brain and he shuddered with lust. This wasn't a good idea. The property was empty, the cove would be deserted, he and Rory would be alone and living together. Whenever he thought of Cap de Mar he thought about sunny days and sensual nights, warm, clear seas and sex…

"You have to go, Mac," Kade said, deeply serious.

Mac knew it was a reasonable option. Hell, he'd brought up the idea of leaving. But he couldn't help feeling like he had as a kid. Powerless over his situation.

"My life sucks," Mac grumbled.

"Yeah, poor baby. You're heading for a luxury house on a Caribbean island with a hot chick." Quinn mocked him by rubbing his eyes like a toddler. "Boo hoo."

Mac still had the use of his good arm. A well-placed punch to Quinn's throat would relieve a lot of his frustration.

Kade ignored Quinn. "I like the idea of you heading to the beach house for all the reasons I mentioned and one more."

"Uh-huh?"

"Nobody will know where you are so you'll be free of the media."

"Always a bonus," Mac agreed.

"And if something happens between you and Rory then they won't pick up on that either," Kade added.

Mac held Kade's mocking glare. Okay, yeah, of course that was a factor. He would try to resist her but his will-power where she was concerned wasn't a sure thing.

"It's not going to happen," he said, but he wasn't sure whether he was trying to convince his friends or himself.

Quinn laughed. "You're going to take one look at Rory in her bikini and be all 'let me show you the view from my room.'"

A punch to the throat would definitely shut Quinn up and would make Mac feel so much better, he mused.

Five

"Sorry, I'm late." Rory picked up her e-reader from her coffee table and shoved it into her tote bag.

"We've got time." Mac, standing by the window, looked at his watch. "Not a lot but some. And if the jet misses its time slot, we'll just request another."

Private jets and time slots. Rory tried not to look impressed. But she was. She was traveling to the Caribbean in *style*. Rory tried to think calmly. She'd done most of her packing last night but she'd thought she'd have time to finish up this morning. Thanks to Troy's mom going walkabout from her nursing home, that hadn't happened. She and Troy had spent three hours looking for her and had eventually tracked her down in a garden center sitting on a bench between two cherry trees. Rory was glad Troy's mom was okay but her temporary disappearance had put a serious dent in Rory's schedule.

"Passport and credit card," Mac told her. "You can buy anything else you need there."

So spoke the man with far too much disposable income, Rory thought. She held up her hand in a silent gesture for him to be quiet. She needed to think, and him standing in her little apartment, looking so hot, wasn't helping. All she could think about was that she was leaving the country with a sexy man who just had to breathe to turn her on.

Her eyes dropped to his arm, which rested in a black sling. He was injured, she reminded herself.

You could go on top...

Rory slapped her hand across her forehead.

"Tell me about Puerto Rico," Rory said, hoping the subject would distract her from thinking about straddling Mac, positioning herself so that...argh!

"It's an island in the Caribbean," Mac replied.

"Don't be a smart-ass. Tell me about the house where we're staying."

Mac leaned his shoulder into the wall and crossed his legs at the ankles. It was so wrong that he looked at home in her apartment, like he had a right to be there. "The house is situated about thirty-five minutes from San Juan, on a secluded cove near only two other houses. It's three stories, mostly open-plan and it has glass folding doors that open up so you feel like you are part of the beach and sea.

"The owners of the other two properties are off-island at the moment so we'll be the *only* people using the cove." Mac added.

Rory swallowed at the low, sexy note in his voice. She'd be alone with Mac, on a Caribbean island, with warm, clear water and white beaches and palm trees.

Utterly and absolutely alone. She wasn't sure whether the appropriate response was to be thrilled or terrified.

Or both.

Sex and business don't mix! He's your patient!

Sun, sea, sexy island…sexy man.

Get a grip, Kydd. Not liking the cocky look in his eyes, the glint that suggested he knew exactly what she was thinking, she lifted her nose. "Well, at least we won't disturb the neighbors with your screams of pain when we start physio."

"Or your screams of pleasure when I make you fall apart in my arms," Mac replied without a second's hesitation.

Rory's heart thumped in her chest but she kept her eyes locked on his, refusing to admit he rattled her. Instead of making her furious, as it should, his comments made her entire body hum in anticipation. Her body was very on board with that idea.

Rory folded her arms and rocked on her heels. "I hate it when you say things like that."

"No, you don't. You want to hate it because it turns you on." Mac looked up at the ceiling. When he looked back at her, his expression was rueful. "Ignore me, ignore that."

She couldn't do as he asked. They needed to address the pole dancing, come-and-get-me-baby elephant gyrating in the room. "Mac, I don't know what you think is going to happen in Puerto Rico, but us sleeping together can't happen, won't happen."

"I know why *I* think it shouldn't happen. I have a few solid reasons for thinking it would be a hell of a mistake, but I'm interested in hearing yours."

Rory bit the inside of her lip. God, she couldn't tell

him she thought he was just like her dad, unfaithful. That the fact he'd dated her sister bugged her. Or her personal favorite: that he drove her crazy.

Rory thought fast and latched onto the first reasonable excuse that popped into her head. "I'm on sticky ground here. I shouldn't treat you and sleep with you—that would be crossing some pretty big lines. I have to maintain professional boundaries with clients. I can't misuse or abuse my position of authority—"

"You have no position of authority over me," Mac scoffed.

"The point remains—" Rory gritted her teeth "—that if I engage in any nonprofessional behavior I can be pulled up before the board."

Mac stared at her, his face inscrutable. "Okay, for the sake of argument, may I point out that you'll be in a foreign country and nobody but us will know? And you're on holiday."

"I'd know," Rory said, her voice resolute. "You might be a rule breaker, Mac, but that's not a risk I'm willing to take."

"You're lying, Rory. Besides, last I checked, physiotherapists are allowed private lives." Mac shook his head. "Not buying it."

So much for using that as an excuse to keep some distance between them. Rory hated the fact that he could look past her cool, professional shell and see below the surface. And he was right. Nobody would believe she'd bullied Mac into having a relationship he didn't want to have. Yeah, sleeping with Mac wouldn't be professional but it wasn't a death sentence either.

She'd forgotten how damn complicated men could be.

"So what is your reason why we shouldn't scratch this particular itch?"

"God, I wish there was just one." Mac dropped a curse and rubbed the back of his neck. "But I can't remember any of them because I am too damn busy thinking about how you taste, how good you feel in my arms. I want to feel that, *feel you*, again. It's not smart, or sensible, but… to hell with being sensible and smart!"

"Mac—"

"Come here, Rorks."

She could say no, should say no, but she found herself walking toward him. Stopping when she was a foot from him, she tipped her head up to look at his face. His jaw held that sexy stubble, and the corners of his mouth suggested he was amused, but his eyes told her everything she needed to know. He was as turned on as she was.

Crazy chemistry.

Mac lifted his good hand, gripped the edge of her collar and pulled her toward him. Rising on her tiptoes, she kept her eyes locked on his, deciding whether she should kiss him or not. "I just want one kiss, Rory," Mac murmured, doing his mind reading thing again. "Stop thinking for a second and *be*."

He had a way of cutting to the heart of the problem. He was right; she was making far too big a deal of this. It didn't have to mean anything! Kissing him just made her feel good. Like chocolate or a foot rub.

"That's it, babe, stop thinking and kiss me."

Rory moved her head so her lips moved across his ear, under his short sideburns, through his surprisingly soft stubble, slowly, so slowly, making her way to his mouth. Mac's hand clenched her waist and she heard the low growl in the back of her throat as her tongue darted out to taste the skin on his jaw, to explore the space where his top and bottom lip met. She felt his erection against her hip and knew she had maybe five seconds before he exploded and all hell—possibly heaven—broke loose.

Rory moved her lips over his, her teeth gently scraping his upper lip, her hand grasping the back of his neck. She kept her tongue away, wondering how long he would wait before he took control of the kiss. Five seconds passed and then another ten. Rory sucked on his bottom lip.

He muttered something against her lips, something harsh and hot and sexy, and his big hand gripped her butt and lifted her up and into him. The time for playing, for teasing, was over. She'd never experienced a kiss so... sexual, Rory realized. This wasn't a prelude to sex. This was just another version of the act. His tongue pushed inside and retreated, swirled and sucked, and Rory felt her panties dampen as she unconsciously ground herself against his erection, frustrated by the layers of fabric between them.

She wanted to get naked. Now.

"Plane waiting. Puerto Rico," Mac muttered after wrenching his mouth off hers.

"You said you could get another time slot and the island isn't going anywhere." Rory snuck her hands under his shirt and scraped her nails across the skin covering the hard muscles of his abs.

"Rory..." Mac muttered a curse and slapped his good hand on hers to keep it from sliding lower. She looked up at him and half smiled at the seventy-shades-of-crazy look on his face. She'd put that look on his face, she thought, amazed. This sexy man looked like he couldn't go without her for one more heartbeat.

"We really should stop," Mac muttered. "We shouldn't take this any further."

"Why not?"

Mac looked rueful. "One reason would be because someone has been pounding on your door for the last minute. At least."

Rory jerked back, surprised. Really? She hadn't heard a damn thing. As the bells in her head stopped ringing she heard the *rat-tat-tat* on her doorjamb. Her heart dropped to the floor; there was only one person who used that particular combination on her door. As a child she'd considered it their secret code, as an adult—about to get lucky—it irritated the hell out of her.

"Problem?" Mac asked as she stepped away from him and pushed a hand into her hair.

"Yes, no...my father." Rory pulled a face. She lifted a hand, waved it toward her front door and grimaced. "Give me a sec, okay?"

Bad timing, Dad, she thought as she crossed the room to the door. Or maybe he'd arrived just in time to save her from making a very silly mistake. Either way, why was he here? She'd called her mother last night, told her that she'd be out of the country for the foreseeable future. Her parents lived in a suburb twenty minutes from here, and since they weren't close, Rory couldn't understand why her father had made the trek to see her.

Rory checked the peephole to make sure it was her father and opened the door. "Dad."

David Kydd had that sheepish look on his face that she was sure had charmed many a woman into his bed over the years. "There's my girl." He leaned forward to kiss her and Rory allowed him to brush her cheek. Since he wasn't one for spontaneous gestures of affection, Rory had to wonder what he was up to.

Okay, she was cynical, but being cynical protected her. She'd learned that if she had no expectations of him then she couldn't be disappointed by his behavior.

"Can I come in?" David asked.

Rory kept her body in the open space of the door so he couldn't look into the apartment and see Mac. Her father was a fan and she didn't want to spend the next hour listening to hockey talk. And, even if she begged him, she wasn't sure her Dad would keep quiet about seeing Mac at her place. Her Dad wasn't the soul of discretion at the best of times.

"It's not a good time. I told Mom last night that I was leaving the city for a while and I need to get to the airport."

"She told me." David gave her another of his sheepish grins. "I thought I'd make the offer to feed your animals or water your plants."

"I don't have pets or plants." As he was well aware. Rory narrowed her eyes at him. "Why are you really here?"

David dropped his eyes and shifted from foot to foot. Eventually he muttered an answer. "Your mother and I are going through a rough time."

Rory felt that familiar, piercing pain shoot through her heart. A rough time… How often had she heard that phrase over the years? *A rough time* meant her mother had caught him again—sexting, cheating, an internet relationship…who knew? He was a master at all of them.

Rory knew how it worked. Her parents would separate for a month or six weeks. Her dad would get bored with his latest conquest and beg her mother to take him back. She liked the begging, liked the attention, and they swore to make it work this time.

"Anyway, we thought that since you wouldn't be here for a while, I could move in to your place until you get back," David suggested, utterly blasé.

"No," Rory told him, her expression brittle. He needed to leave her, and her apartment, out of any games he was playing.

Rory stepped backward and rubbed her forehead with her fingertips. "I've got to go. I'm late as it is."

"Rory, come on," David pleaded.

"Sorry." Rory closed the door in his face and rested her forehead against the wood, trying to hold back the tears threatening to fall. She needed a minute to find her center, to process what had just happened.

She heard her father's footsteps as he walked away from her door. There went the reason why she found it difficult, impossible really, to trust that someone she allowed herself to love would not lie to her or abandon her. How could she put her faith in love after witnessing her parents' skewed perception of the emotion all her life? As a product of their twisted love, was she even worthy of being in a monogamous relationship? If such a thing even existed.

She was so damn confused about the meaning of love and marriage. Why did her parents stay together after all this drama? What did they get out of it? Their love, their marriage, their entire married life had been a sham, an illusion…

Love was a sham, an illusion…

"Rorks? You okay?"

Dammit. She'd temporarily forgotten Mac was in the room. He'd witnessed that silly conversation. She turned slowly. How could she explain this without going into the embarrassing details? She managed to find a smile, unaware that it didn't come anywhere near her eyes. "Sorry about that." She made herself laugh. "My folks, slightly touched."

Mac's skeptical look told her he didn't buy her breezy attitude. Yet there was something in his eyes that suggested sympathy, that made her want to confide in him, to tell him why her parents drove her batty. She had the strange idea that he might understand.

Rory bit the inside of her cheek, confused and feeling off-kilter. Since meeting Mac again, her life had done a one-eighty. She felt like she was standing in a fun house. The reflections didn't make sense...

"Excuse me a sec," Rory said before walking through her bedroom to the bathroom. Grabbing the counter in an iron-fisted grip, she stared at herself in the mirror.

What was she doing? Thinking? She simply wasn't sure and she wished she had more than five minutes to figure it out. This thing between her and Mac was getting out of hand, and she needed, more than anything, to control it, to understand it.

She was about to fly away with him and how was she going to resist him?

It was just sex, she told herself. Sex was physical. It wasn't a promise to hand over her heart. If she slept with Mac she would be sharing her body, not her soul, and she wouldn't be risking anything emotional. Could she be laid-back about such an intimate act? She would have to be, because love wasn't an option. She wasn't interested, and Mac wasn't the type of guy a girl should risk her heart on anyway.

But...

But it would be cleaner, smarter, less complicated if she didn't sleep with him. Passion and chemistry like theirs was crazy. Her libido was acting like a wild and uncontrollable genie. A genie who would be impossible to get back in the bottle if she popped the cork. It was far better to keep the situation, and her lust, contained.

Rory pointed her index finger at her reflection and scowled. "Do not let him pop your cork, Kydd."

In his seat, Mac scowled at his computer screen through his wire-rimmed glasses and wished he could concentrate. He needed to make sense of these balance sheets and read the profit and loss statements for a couple of sports bars they owned in Toronto. How was he supposed to do that when his mind was filled with Rory? He turned his head sideways to look at her and smiled when he saw she'd curled up in her seat and fallen asleep. He picked up a lock of hair that had fallen over her eyes and gently tucked it behind her ear.

So much more beautiful than she'd been at nineteen.

Mac pulled off his glasses and rubbed his eyes, conscious of the fiery throb in his arm. His head ached in sympathy. Truth be told, he was relieved to be leaving the city and to stop pretending he was fine. He could take the pain tablets, zone out and try not to worry about Myra and the investor and the fans and, God, whether the press would find out how serious his injury actually was and how much pain he was living with.

Rory let out a breathy sigh and he looked at her again, his stomach churning with the need to have her. That need worried him.

With her, he didn't feel in control and he hated that sensation. In his real life, he dated to get laid. He and the woman both had fun and then they moved on. He understood how much it hurt to have unmet expectations so he made no promises, offered no hope to the women who slept with him. In his world, sex didn't involve talking, sharing, caring. In that world, conversation took place horizontally; bodies spoke, not mouths.

He didn't confide in any of his lovers. He never shared his feelings, and the one guarantee his lovers had was that he'd always leave.

He never allowed anyone to get too close; he'd learned a long time ago to be his own champion, his own motivator. His mother hadn't believed in or supported him so he didn't expect anyone else to either.

Rory was different. She made him feel more, made him say more, want more. He was out of his depth with her and flailing...

Mac rubbed his temples with his fingertips. He was definitely losing it. *Flailing? Over a woman?* God, he sounded like a fool.

Irritated with himself and his introspection, he picked up his tablet computer and swiped his finger across the screen, immediately hitting the link for his favorite news site. Instead of focusing on the US elections or the migrant crisis in Europe, the headlines detailed the breakup of a famous Hollywood golden couple after ten years and fostering six kids.

Mac had been caught in the same type of media hype, on less of a global scale admittedly, and it had sucked.

Phoenix is currently being treated for depression and begs the media to give her some privacy, he read. He'd heard that Shay had suffered with depression during their breakup and the constant press attention had made the situation ten times worse. He couldn't do that to Rory, couldn't risk her like that. Yeah, it was Puerto Rico. Yes, they would be flying under the radar. But it just took one determined paparazzo, one photograph, and their world would implode.

Not happening. He had to keep his hands off her.

"You look like your brain is going to explode," Rory softly said.

Mac rolled his head on his shoulders and watched as she stretched. "It feels that way," he admitted, knowing he had to address this longing for her. Now or never, he thought.

You won't die if you don't have sex. You might think you are going to, but you won't.

Mac rubbed his temples again. "Look, Rory, I've been thinking."

Rory sent him an uncertain look. "Uh-huh?"

"Despite my smart comments about us sleeping together and that hot kiss, maybe it would be better if we didn't. Sleep together, that is."

He couldn't help noticing the immediate flash of relief in her eyes. So something had shifted in her after that bizarre conversation with her father. When she'd returned from the bathroom, sexy Rory had disappeared and had been replaced with enigmatic Rory. He still didn't know what to make of that.

"Want to clue me in on why you've had a change of heart?"

You scare the crap out of me? When I'm with you I feel like I am on shifting sand? I don't want to see you hurt or scared or feeling hunted?

Yeah, he couldn't admit to any of the above.

So he fudged the truth. "My arm is killing me. I'd like to get to the house and chill, take my meds and just zone out for a while. I want to relax and not have to worry about you or keeping you happy, in bed or out." Mac stared past her to look out the window. "I'd like us to play it cool, just be friends." Because he was a man and believed in keeping his options open, he tacked on a proviso. "For now?"

Rory didn't answer, her gray eyes contemplative. "Sure. Fine."

Mac watched her out of the corner of his eye and sighed. *Fine.* God, he hated that word, especially when a woman stated it in that hard-to-read way. What did it actually mean? Was she okay with waiting? Was she pissed? Did she actually want to say "Screw you"?

Sometimes, most times, women made no sense. At all.

Six

Rory loved the Cap de Mar beach house. Shortly after her arrival, she claimed one of the smaller guest rooms, partly because it had an excellent view of the U-shaped bay and mostly because it was a floor below and a long way from the massive master suite.

She pulled on a bikini, a pair of shorts and a T-shirt and, walking barefoot, she set out to explore the house. As Mac had said, the living areas, sitting and dining room and the kitchen were all open-plan, leading onto a massive balcony filled with comfortable chairs and day-beds either under the balcony roof or under umbrellas. Tucked into the corner of the balcony was a huge Jacuzzi and she could easily imagine sitting in that tub watching the sun go down.

It was mid-afternoon now, Rory thought, resting her elbows on the railing and looking down into the sparkling pool below her. In a perfect world she'd like to take a swim, lie in the sun and then sit on the beach with a glass of white wine in her hand and wait for the sun to paint the horizon in Day-Glo colors. That, she thought, would be a wonderful end to a rather difficult day…

Rory saw a movement out of the corner of her eye and saw Mac step out of his bedroom through the doors that led straight onto this balcony. He'd shucked his jeans and shirt and pulled on a pair of board shorts. He hadn't bothered with a shirt. Why should he? He had a torso to die for.

The rest of him was pretty spectacular too.

Rory huffed out a sigh. She had to corral her overexcited hormones. Speaking of hormones, she'd been caught flat-footed at Mac's suggestion they postpone sleeping together. She hadn't expected Mac would let his arm get in the way of pleasure, or that he was humble enough to admit he was in pain and needed some time.

Mac, barefoot, walked over and gestured to the cove. "Nice, isn't it?"

"Gorgeous," Rory agreed. "It almost feels like we are part of the beach."

Mac half smiled. "That was the intention when I designed it. I wanted to bring the outdoors in."

"You designed this?"

Mac sat down on a daybed and leaned back, placing his good hand under his head. His biceps bulged, his shoulder flexed and the rest of him rippled as he swung his legs up onto the cushions. "Yeah."

She remembered something about him and architecture, about studying it in college. When he was dating Shay, he'd just completed some business courses and Rory had been super impressed that he'd managed to study and still play for the Mavericks. He hadn't needed to study further; he was earning enough with his salary and endorsements that, if he invested it properly, he could live comfortably for a very long time.

This wasn't living comfortably, Rory thought, looking around. This was living large. An island home on a secluded beach translated into big-boy money. She recalled what Troy had said about him and his friends investing in property and businesses, and her curiosity had her asking, "How many properties do you own? How many businesses do you have?"

Mac looked at her from below half-closed eyes. "Enough." He yawned and dropped his arm to pick up a pillow and shove it behind his head. "You want a statement of my assets and liabilities, Rory?"

Rory flushed. Okay, admittedly, she had no right to ask him that; they weren't lovers. They weren't even friends. And she'd rather die than ask any of her other clients such a personal question.

"Kade, Quinn and I have our own projects but a lot of our assets are held together in a partnership, and all the assets we share have to generate an income, this house included. It's our rule. If it doesn't make money, we ditch it. That is why we get to use this property but, for the most part, it's rented out. Not so much during the summer months because it's so damn hot and it's hurricane season."

Rory darted a quick look toward the endlessly blue horizon. "Hurricanes?"

"They happen," Mac replied. "They aren't that bad. A lot of wind, a lot of rain."

"Super," Rory said drily.

Mac shifted in his seat and winced when he moved his injured arm, trying to find a more comfortable position.

"Did you take your painkillers and the anti-inflammatory pills?" Rory demanded.

"Yes, Mom, that's why I'm feeling so damn sleepy," Mac murmured. He waved a hand toward the house. "Food and drinks in the kitchen. I asked our rental agent to arrange for someone to stock the place. I've also arranged for someone to come and clean and do laundry a couple of times a week. Otherwise we're on our own."

On our own was a phrase she did not need to hear.

"Okay," Rory said, watching him fight sleep.

"Jeep in the garage. Keys in the kitchen. San Juan is thirty-five minutes away, north. Casinos, restaurants five minutes away, south." Mac yawned again. "Make yourself at home."

"Will do," Rory said, but she doubted he'd heard her because he'd drifted off to sleep. He still had a frown on his face as she moved an umbrella closer to him so he could sleep in the shade. Her thumb moved over the creases on his forehead and she wondered what was making him worry. Their deal to buy the Mavericks franchise, his injury, being alone with Rory in this house?

She might have her fair share of problems but Mac had his too.

He wasn't always who she expected him to be, Rory admitted. Sure, he could be overconfident about his abilities and about the effect he had on her, but he was also honest enough to admit that their attraction was a two-way street. She affected him just as badly. She didn't know Mac well, not yet, and because he was so damn reticent, she probably never would. But she did know he wasn't the arrogant jerk he'd been ten years ago. He was ambitious and determined, but he wasn't selfish. He was smart and loyal and, yes, infuriating.

It was a surprise to realize that she *liked* him. A lot. And that liking had nothing to do with his masculine face and sculpted muscles.

There was a great deal more to Mac McCaskill than his pretty packaging. Dammit.

With every conversation they shared he shattered another of her preconceptions. If they continued these conversations, she'd start to like him a little more than she should, and there was a possibility she would feel more for him than lust and attraction.

She couldn't let that happen. She would have to try to ignore him, try to avoid him. Because falling in lust with him was one thing, falling in *like* with him was another.

Falling in love with him would be intolerable.

So she simply wouldn't.

A week after landing in San Juan, Rory and Mac watched the sun go down in the small fishing village of Las Croabas. She was full to bursting from demolishing a massive bowl of crab seviche. She was relaxed and a little buzzy. The single glass of wine couldn't be blamed for that, she thought. No, it was a combination of the spectacular sunset—God was painting the sky with vivid purples and iridescent oranges—and the equally magnificent man who sat opposite her, hair ruffled by the balmy evening breeze.

A lovely sunset, a rustic restaurant, a really hot guy with a girl eating dinner…they could be an advertisement for romance, Rory thought. There would be no truth in that advertisement. Mac hadn't laid a finger on her since they'd arrived in Puerto Rico and he hadn't kissed her again. Truthfully, she hadn't given him any opportunity to do either as she'd made a point of spending as little time with him as she possibly could without shirking her duties.

But a girl had to eat, and over dinner she'd intercepted a couple of intense looks from him, which made her think he'd catch her if she decided to jump him.

Which she wouldn't. But the will-he-won't-he anticipation was, admittedly, very hot and incredibly sexy.

"There's something I have to tell you," Mac said.

That sounded ominous, Rory thought. "What is it?"

"There's a hurricane on the way." He lifted his seviche-filled fork to his mouth.

"A big one?" she squawked, half lifting her butt off her seat and whipping around to inspect the horizon. It was still cloud-free. Shouldn't there be clouds?

Mac shrugged. "Big enough."

"How big is *big enough*?" Rory demanded. How could he eat? A natural phenomena was about to smack them in the face. "When will it arrive? Should we evacuate? Are there bunkers?"

Mac sent her a puzzled glance. "It's a hurricane, not a nuclear bomb, Rorks."

"You're not giving me any information!" Rory wailed. She tried to recall what she'd read about preparing for a hurricane and, unfortunately, it wasn't a lot. Or anything at all. "Don't we need to put boards up or something?"

"I've arranged to have some guys come over tomorrow to put the boards up. Stupid, because I could do them if it wasn't for this arm!"

"I'm sure I can do it," Rory bravely suggested. She didn't know if she could but she thought she should offer.

Mac smiled at her. "No offense, Rorks, but it'll take them a couple of hours and it would take you two weeks."

"Why do people always say 'no offense' and then go on to offend you?" Rory grumbled.

"How often have you wielded a hammer?"

Rory lifted her nose at his smirk. "I pound in my own hooks to hang pictures." Well, she had once and had lost a fingernail in the process. Troy then banned her from using tools. He'd fixed her cupboard door, replaced the broken tile in her shower, fixed the leaky pipe under her sink. Troy also changed the tires on her car, made a mean chicken parmesan and removed spiders. He'd be her perfect husband if he only liked girls. And if she was even marginally attracted to him.

"Liar," Mac said cheerfully.

His ability to see through her annoyed the pants off her. Actually, the way he looked, his deep voice, his laugh—all of it made her want to drop her pants, but that was another story entirely. "Tell me about the hurricane!"

Mac dug his fork into his salad. "I'm not sure what you want to know. There's a hurricane approaching. It'll probably hit land around midnight tomorrow night. There will be wind, rain. We'll be fine."

Rory scowled at him. "You are so annoying."

Mac's lips twitched. "I try." He dumped some wine into their glasses, picked hers up and handed it to her. "Drink. We might as well enjoy the gorgeous night before we die."

Rory rolled her eyes. "If you're going to be a smart-ass, there has to be some smart involved. Otherwise you just sound like an ass." She took the glass from his hand, looked into his amused eyes and sighed. "I'm overreacting, aren't I?"

Mac lifted his glass to his lips, sipped and swallowed. "Just a little." He sent her another quick, quirky smile. "We'll be fine. If I thought we were in danger, I'd be making arrangements to get you out of here."

Rory nodded and took a large sip of her wine. Okay, then. Maybe she could cope with the hurricane. She glanced at the sky. "Tomorrow night, huh?"

Mac lifted his hand and rubbed his thumb across her bottom lip. He lingered there, pressing the fullness before moving from her lip and drifting up and over her cheekbone. She watched as his eyes deepened, turned a blue-black in the early evening light. Rory tossed a look at the beach and wished she could jump up from the table and walk—run—away.

She'd been doing that for the last week, finding any excuse to avoid him. She left his presence when she felt the spit drying up in her mouth, when she felt the first throb between her legs. Because Mac spent most of his time shirtless, she'd spent a lot of time walking away from him. She'd run to the beach, run *on* the beach, had started canoeing and snorkeling again. She'd also taken a lot of cold showers.

She was *so* pathetic.

"You can't run off in the middle of a meal," Mac told her, his eyes dancing.

Rory lifted her nose and tried to look puzzled. "Sorry?"

"You've been avoiding me, running away every time something sparks between us," Mac said conversationally, dropping his hand from her face and popping an olive from his salad into his mouth.

"Uh—"

"You're not alone. Every time you do therapy on me,

I have to stop myself from grabbing you and kissing you senseless."

Rory groaned and dropped her chin to her chest.

Mac twisted his fingers in hers. "Your hands touch me and I inhale your scent—you smell so damn good—and my brain starts to shut down. It's not just you, Rory."

Rory picked up her glass and sipped, trying to get some moisture back into her mouth. "Ah... I'm not sure what to say."

"Avoiding each other makes it worse. It's driving me crazy. I barely sleep at night because I want you in my bed." Mac's voice raised goose bumps all over her skin. "What are we going to do about this...situation, Rory?"

Rory touched the top of her lip with the tip of her tongue and her eyelids dropped to half-mast. Couldn't he see the big fat take-me-now sign blazing from her forehead in flashing neon?

She blew out a breath and sent him a rueful shrug. Mac seemed to have a hard time taking his eyes off her mouth. He was enjoying the anticipation, too, she realized when his gaze slammed into hers, his eyes hot and filled with passion.

"How the hell am I supposed to resist you?" he demanded.

Rory rolled her shoulders and gripped his wrist.

"I don't do relationships," Mac growled.

"I don't either," Rory softly replied. "But I can't stop wondering whether we'll be as good together as all the kisses we've shared suggest."

Mac shot up and with one step he was standing in front of her and pulling her to her feet. Keeping his injured arm hanging at his side, he used his other arm to yank her into his hard chest. His mouth slammed against hers.

His tongue slid once, then twice over her lips, and she immediately opened her mouth and allowed him inside. He tasted of wine and sex and heat, and Rory pushed into him so she could feel her nipples touch his chest through the thin fabric of their cotton shirts. She sighed when his erection nudged her stomach, and she linked her hands at the back of his neck to stop herself from reaching down and encircling him. Kissing in a public place was one thing, but heavy petting was better done in a more private setting.

"You taste so damn good," Mac muttered against her lips, his hand sliding over her butt. "And you feel even better."

"Kiss me again," Rory demanded, tipping her head to the side so he could change the angle of the kiss, go deeper and wetter.

"If I kiss you again I don't know if I'm gonna be able to stop," Mac replied, resting his forehead on hers.

"Who asked you to?"

Mac half laughed and half groaned. "You're not helping, Rorks." He stepped back and pushed her hair, curly from the humidity, from her eyes. "Let's take a step back here, think about this a little more. Make damn sure it's what we want."

Rory glanced down, saw the evidence of his want and lifted an eyebrow. "We both want it, McCaskill."

"Yeah, but what we want is not always good for us," Mac said, suddenly somber. He picked up her hand and rubbed the ball of his thumb across her knuckles. "We're here for a little while longer, Rory. I don't want to muck this up. There are consequences."

"I'm on the pill and I expect you to use a condom."

"Noted. But those aren't the consequences I'm worrying about."

Rory cocked her head. "Okay, what are you talking about?"

"I don't want either of us to regret this in the morning, to feel awkward, to feel we've made a colossal mistake." Mac looked uncharacteristically unsure of himself as he tugged at the collar of his white linen button-down shirt. "Taking you to bed would be easy, Rory. Making love to you would be a pleasure. In the morning we're both still going to be here. You still need to treat me and we have to live together. I don't want it to get weird between us."

Those were all fair points. "Anything else?"

Mac looked around them, frowned and rocked on his heels. "We're flying under the radar here but if just one person sees us, snaps a photo—we're toast. If it gets out that you're my physio, or that we're sleeping together and you are my ex's sister, it'll be news."

She hauled in a sharp breath. Wow, she hadn't even considered that.

"The media will go nuts and you'll be at the center of it, like Shay was," Mac added.

The thought made her want to heave. She'd never felt comfortable in the limelight and couldn't think of anything worse than being meat for the media's grinder.

"They will wonder why you—the best physiotherapist around—are treating me and why are you doing it in secret. They'll dig until they find out the truth," Mac said.

Rory dropped her head to look at the floor.

"Are you prepared to risk all that, Rory? Can you deal with the consequences of the worst-case scenario?"

"It won't happen." Rory bit her bottom lip.

"Probably not, but what if it does? Can you deal?"

"Can you?" Rory demanded. "You have more to lose than I do."

"Yeah, don't think that I haven't realized that," Mac muttered, and pinched the bridge of his nose with his finger and thumb. When he opened his eyes, she saw the ruefulness, the touch of amusement, in his gaze.

"Yet I still want you. I'm really hoping to get over it," he added. His tone invited her to help him break the tension, to get over this awkward, emotion-tinged moment. He picked up his wineglass, drained the contents and looked at his empty glass. "See, you're driving me to drink."

Rory bumped her wineglass against his. "I feel your pain. You should try living inside my head."

Mac dropped a quick, hard kiss on her mouth. "Help me out and be sensible about this, Rorks. I'm relying on you to be the adult here because I have little or no sense when it comes to wanting you."

Well, that comment didn't help!

Seven

The next day Rory stood on the beach in front of the house and knew Mac was watching her from the balcony, his good hand gripping the railing, his expression brooding. She tilted her face up and looked for the sun, now hidden behind gloomy, dark clouds. She'd been, maybe obsessively, glued to the Weather Channel, and she knew the hurricane was about twelve hours away. It would slam into them later tonight.

The wind had already picked up and was whipping her hair around her head and pushing her sarong against her thighs. The sea, normally gentle, was choppy and rough, and foam whipped across the surface of the ocean. It looked nothing like the warm friend who had been sharing his delights and treasures with her on a daily basis.

Everything was changing, Rory thought. She picked a piece of seaweed off her ankle, tossed it and watched the wind whisk it away. Like she'd have to face the hurricane, she couldn't run away from Mac anymore. She couldn't hide. She couldn't avoid him or the passion he whipped up in her.

He was right, she had a choice to make…hell, she'd already made the choice. She knew it. He knew it… If she gave him the slightest hint, like breathing, he'd do her in a New York minute.

What she had to do now was stand strong and ride the winds, hoping she'd come out with as little damage as possible when it all ended. Her desire—no, her *need*—for him was too strong, too compelling. She just had to ride the crazy as best she could and hope she could stop the lines between lust and like—she absolutely refused to use any other *L* word—from smudging together.

She turned and looked back at the house and across the sand, across the shrubs that separated the beach from his house, their eyes met. Even at a distance she could see and feel his desire for her, knew that hers was in her heated eyes, on her face, in every gesture she made.

She couldn't run away anymore so she ran to him, into that other hurricane rapidly bearing down on her, one that was even scarier than the one approaching from the sea.

She couldn't wait another second, another minute. Her resistance had petered out. Her need for him was greater than her desire to protect herself. This was it, this was now…

Rory picked up the trailing ends of her sarong and pulled the fabric up above her knees and belted across the sand. The wind tossed her hair into her eyes and she grabbed the strands blowing in her face, holding them out of her eyes so she could watch Mac, watch for that moment when he realized she wasn't running away from the storm but running to him, running into the tempest she knew she'd find in his touch.

He wasn't an idiot so he caught on pretty quickly. She knew it by the way he straightened, the way his appreciative glance became predatory, anticipatory. But he just stood on the balcony, waiting for her to fly to him. She knew he was waiting for her to change her mind, like she'd been doing, to avoid the steps that led from the path directly to where he was standing. He was expecting her to veer off and enter the house, access her room via the second set of stairs farther along.

She wanted to yell at him that she wouldn't change her mind, that she wanted him intensely, crazily, without thought. She hurtled up the steps and bolted onto the balcony, skidding to a stop when he leaned his hip against the railing and jammed his hand into the pocket of his expensive khaki shorts.

What if she'd read the situation wrong? What if he'd changed his mind? Rory flushed with embarrassment and dropped her gaze, looking at her cherry-red toes. She'd picked the color because she thought it was vibrant, sexy, because she could imagine him taking her baby toe, exquisitely sensitive and tipped with red, into his hot mouth…

Rory let out a small moan and closed her eyes.

"You okay?" Mac asked, and when she heard the amusement in his voice she flushed again. God, she must look like an idiot. She *was* an idiot.

"Fine."

Mac's penetrating gaze met hers. "On the beach, you made a decision."

She rocked on her heels. "Yep."

"You're sure?"

"Yep."

He didn't move toward her. Was he waiting for her to make the first move? Unsure, it had been so damn long since she'd danced this dance, she looked around for a temporary distraction because she had no idea what to do, to say. "Storm is on its way."

Mac's eyes didn't leave her face. "I know. Are you scared?"

Of this? Of liking you too much? Of making a mistake? Absolutely terrified.

"I'm a hurricane virgin," she admitted, trying for a light tone but hearing only her croaky voice.

"I have a plan to distract you," Mac softly stated, moving so he stood so close to her that his chest brushed her cotton shirt. He pushed his thigh between her legs as he placed his wineglass on the table next to him. "But in order for the distraction to work we have to practice, often."

Rory closed her eyes in relief and smiled. "Really? It'll have to be very good to distract me from the storm."

"That's why we have to practice." Mac placed his hand on her hip, sliding it under the fabric of her sarong, his hand making contact with the bare skin at her waist. Rory looked at his mouth and stood on her toes, reaching up so her lips met his. His mouth softened, his eyes closed and his long lashes became smudges on his cheeks. She felt him holding back, felt the tension as his mouth rested on hers, as if he were savoring the moment, taking stock. She placed her hand on his waist and flicked her tongue out to trace his lips, to encourage him to let go, to come out and play.

Mac exploded. His good arm went around her back and she was pulled flush against him as his mouth plundered hers in a kiss that was all heat and passion and pent-up frustration. His tongue twisted around hers and his hand pushed the fabric of her sarong down her hips. The knot in the fabric impeded his progress. He pulled back and hissed in frustration.

"You're going to have to help me, honey," he said, his voice rough and growly. He swore. "I want to rip everything off you but that's not gonna happen. Get naked, please?"

Rory, her hands now linked around his neck, dropped her head back so she could look into his frustrated face. Against her stomach she felt the hard, long line of his erection and she noticed the fine tremors skittering under his skin. He was half insane with wanting her and she liked him like that. Maybe she could drive him a little crazier...

It would be fun to try. "I think you need to get naked first," she said, stepping back.

"Uh, no." Mac gripped the hand that started to undo the buttons on his shirt. "If that happens then this is going to be over a lot sooner than we'd like."

Rory placed a kiss on the *V* just below his throat. "I'm not going to let that happen. I intend to go very, very slowly." She carried on with separating the buttons from their holes and then she pushed the sides of his shirt apart and placed her hands on his pecs, his flat nipples underneath her palms. Mac's hand reached between them to echo her movement by placing his hand on her breast.

"No bare skin," he complained.

Rory reached for her thin cotton shirt and pulled it over her head to reveal her strapless bikini top. Allowing him a moment to look, she pushed his shirt off his shoulder and gently maneuvered the shirt down his hurt arm, dropping kisses on the still-bruised skin. "You sure you can do this?" she murmured, her mouth against his biceps.

"My arm hurts, not the rest of me. Well, another part of me is aching, too, but in the best way possible." He tugged at the edge of her tangerine bikini top, looking impatient. "Take this off. Take it all off."

Rory reached behind her with one hand and undid the snap. The top fell forward and Mac pulled the fabric down, and she allowed it to drop to the ground as she watched him peruse her. His fingers drifted over her already puckered nipples and she sucked in a breath when he dropped his head so that his lips closed over her in a deep, seductive kiss.

She could feel her nipple on the roof of his mouth and shuddered as his tongue swept over her, once, twice. She was supposed to be making him crazy, she thought, yet he was the one pushing her. Dropping her head back, she threaded one hand into his hair to hold him in place as he put one knee on the daybed next to him to align his mouth perfectly with her chest. Moving away, he dropped a hot kiss onto her sternum before turning his mouth to the neglected nipple on her other breast. Rory pulled the knot of her sarong apart and pushed her bikini bottoms down her hips, forgetting about them as they fell to the floor.

She felt Mac stiffen as he looked down. What would he see? A flat stomach with a faded appendix scar, a narrow landing strip and short legs? She'd far prefer he touch rather than look.

"Mac," she groaned. God, she'd waited ten long years for him to touch her there yet he kept his forehead between her breasts, huffing like a freight train.

"Getting there," Mac muttered. "God, you're gorgeous. I could look at you forever."

"I'd prefer you use your hands and mouth," Rory told him, pushing his hand between her legs. She couldn't wait, she was burning with need.

Mac's hard, knowing fingers found her bud and had her arching her back. She felt the insistent throbbing that told her she was so very close to losing it. It took one sliding finger and she was exploding, bucking, sobbing and laughing, tumbling along that fantastically ferocious wave of pure, cosmic pleasure.

When her pleasure tapered off, leaving her lady parts still tingling, she realized she was half sitting on Mac's thighs, his mouth was on her breast and his erection was tenting his pants. Climbing off him, she helped him push his shorts over his hips so he was free to her touch. She wrapped her hands around him and smiled at his shudder and desperate groan.

He pulled her hands away one at a time and held her wrists behind her back with one hand. "I'm so close. If you squeeze me once…"

Rory shrugged. "Not a problem." Actually, she'd love to see him lose control.

"Hell, no," Mac said, dropping his lips to pull the skin beneath her ear. "I want to be inside you. I need to be inside you."

"Okay," Rory told him, her hand drifting across his eight-pack. "God, you have the most amazing body."

His erection jumped at her words and his mouth slammed onto hers. Pulling her down to the daybed, he lay on his back and Rory flung a leg over him, immediately settling her happy spot on his hard shaft. She was going to come again. Woo-hoo, lucky her.

"Condom," she gasped, needing him to slide on home.

Mac lifted his hips and pushed his hand under the cushion next to his thigh. He cursed when he came up empty.

"Try the other side," he huffed, and Rory leaned sideways to pat the space under the cushion. Feeling the cool foil packets, she pulled a condom loose, and instead of one, she held a four-pack in her hand. She looked down and then lifted an eyebrow in Mac's direction.

"Confident, aren't you?" she asked.

"Prepared. I have them stashed all over the house," Mac admitted, grabbing a condom and lifting the packet to his teeth to open it. He cursed at his clumsiness and Rory took it from him.

"So, when did you put the packet of condoms there, McCaskill?" she asked as she rolled the latex down his shaft.

Mac grinned. "Ten minutes after we arrived. Though, to be fair, I've had this fantasy about making love to you since the day we met."

Rory jerked at his words. Which time? Years ago or weeks ago? Then the questions disappeared as Mac pushed into her, stretching and filling and completing her.

She rose and fell, easily matching his rhythm. He filled her cold and empty spaces, she thought, as he speared up into her. She glanced down and saw him watching her, his eyes deep and dark and determined. "Come for me, baby."

Not able to refuse him, Rory shattered around him, and from a place far away she felt his last thrust, felt him pulse against her as her followed her over the cliff.

Rory collapsed against his chest. His good arm wrapped around her as she turned her face into his neck.

She inhaled the scents of the fragrant, perfumed air and sex, felt his thumping heart beneath hers, the rough texture of his chest hair beneath her cheek.

This place, here in his embrace, was the place she felt safest. Happiest. The place she most wanted to be.

Dammit.

Mac had always liked hurricanes. The power extreme weather contained was thrilling. He'd experienced two storms on the island before and neither had done much damage. He expected this storm would be more of the same.

He stood on the veranda and watched the sky darken. The wind was picking up and he mentally took inventory of his hurricane supplies. They had enough water and food for three days, adequate lighting for when the power went off and he had, and knew how to use, his extensive first-aid kit. They were ready for the storm; the boards were up courtesy of a couple of young guys from the village who'd made short work of the task. They'd also moved the outside furniture into the store rooms next to the garage and generally made themselves useful. They would be fine and if it was just him, he'd jump into bed with a good book and let the storm do its thing, but Rory was acting like it was the hour before the world ended. He turned his head and saw that she sat where he'd left her, in the corner of the couch, her arms clutching a pillow in a death grip, her eyes wide and scared.

"Relax, we'll be fine," he told her.

"We're on the edge of a beach with a hurricane approaching...which means big waves and big wind. I think I've got a right to panic," Rory retorted. "Will you please come inside?"

Mac lifted his face to the sky, enjoying the rain-tinged wind on his face. "I built this house to be, as much as possible, hurricane-proof."

"Don't you have a shelter?"

"That's for tornadoes, not hurricanes." Mac told her, walking back into the room. He lifted a bottle of wine and aimed the opening at her glass. "Have some wine, try to relax."

"Huh." Rory gulped from her glass and her anxious eyes darted to the rapidly darkening sky.

He needed to distract her or else she'd soon be a basket case. The wind howled and the lights flickered. Rory pushed herself farther into the corner of the couch. He sat down next to her, put his feet up onto the coffee table and placed his hand on her thigh beneath the edge of her shorts. More sex would be a great distraction, he thought, but Rory's white face and tense body suggested she might kick him if he proposed that. Besides, they'd done it three times since noon. She needed some time to recover.

And that meant talking. Dammit. Not his best talent. Maybe he'd get lucky and she'd start.

He was given a temporary reprieve when his cell phone buzzed. Picking it up, he saw a message from Quinn, checking whether they were okay, and he quickly replied. He picked up Rory's cell phone and tossed it into her lap. "I suggest you let your friends and family know there is a hurricane and you are safe. They tend to freak if you don't. And the cell towers sometimes go down during storms so we might lose our signal."

Rory nodded quickly and her fingers flew across the keypad. Within thirty seconds her phone buzzed and she was smiling at the message on the screen. "It's Shay, suggesting I climb under a bed with a bottle of vodka."

Shay...now there was a subject they'd been avoiding. He sipped his wine and rested his head on the back of the couch. "Did you take flak because we almost kissed?"

Rory tapped her finger against her glass. "You have no idea. She refused to talk to me for six months and it took us a while to find our groove again."

Mac frowned. "Look, I admit I wasn't exactly Prince Charming that night, I messed up in numerous ways but, God, we were young, and nothing happened!" Mac waited a beat. "Even if that open-mic incident hadn't happened, she knew we were on our way out—"

"She'd mentioned she thought she was approaching her expiry date," Rory interjected, her voice dry.

Mac winced. "Look, I can understand her thinking I'm a douche, but why couldn't she forgive you?"

Rory's eyes flicked to his face and went back to studying her wine. "The reason why Shay has such massive insecurities and the reason why I am not good at relationships is the same."

Wait. Why would she think that she wasn't good at relationships? She was open and friendly and funny and smart, who wouldn't want to be in a relationship with her? Well, he wouldn't...but he didn't want to be in a relationship with anyone so he didn't count. She had to be better at relationships than he was; then again, pretty much ninety percent of the world's population was. "How do you know that you are bad at relationships?"

Rory's laugh was brittle. She looked him in the eye and tried, unsuccessfully, to smile. "I can date, I can flirt, I can do light and fluffy, but I suck at commitment. I drive men crazy."

He couldn't imagine it. Here he was, the King of Easily Bored, and he was as entranced with Rory as he'd been from the beginning. "How?"

Rory waved his question away. "When I think things are getting hot or heavy or too much to deal with—when I get scared—I take the easy way out and I run. I just disappear."

There was a message in her statement and he was smart enough to hear it. When she thought their time was over she'd make like Casper and fade away. Good to know, he thought cynically. Thinking back, he remembered what she'd said earlier. "You said there was a reason why you and Shay act like you do. Will you tell me what it is?"

He was as surprised as she looked at his question. He hadn't intended to ask that. Did he really want to know the answer? It seemed he did, he reluctantly admitted. Rory was, when she let go, naturally warm and giving, and he wondered why she felt the need to protect herself.

"Well, that's a hell of a subject to discuss during a hurricane," Rory replied, tucking her feet under her. "Actually, it's a hell of a subject at any time."

"We can talk about something else, if you prefer." Mac backtracked to give her, and him, an out of the conversation. He stood and walked over to the open balcony doors, holding his flashlight in his hand. Unable to resist the power of the approaching storm, he stepped outside and let the rapidly increasing wind slam into him. He leaned forward, surprised that the wind could hold him upright as the rain smacked his face like icy bullets.

Hello, Hurricane Des, Mac thought as he stepped back into the house and closed and bolted the doors behind him. The lights flickered and he checked that the hurricane lamp and matches were on the coffee table. They would probably lose power sooner rather than later. Mac resumed his seat, linked his hands across his stomach and looked at Rory. "Want to talk about something else?"

Rory shrugged and pulled the tassels of the pillow through nervous fingers. He knew it wasn't only the crazy wind slamming into the house that made her nervous. The power dropped, surged and died.

"Perfect," Rory muttered.

Within a minute Mac had the hurricane lamps casting a gentle glow across the room and smiled at Rory's relieved sigh. "My parents are hugely dysfunctional..."

"Aren't they all?"

Rory cocked an eyebrow at his interruption but he gestured for her to continue. "When I was thirteen, I was in the attic looking for an old report card—I wanted to show Shay that I was better at math than she was." Rory tipped her head. "Strange that I remember that... Anyway, I was digging in an old trunk when I found photographs of my father with a series of attractive women." Rory pushed her hair back with one hand. Her eyes looked bleak. "It didn't take me long to realize those photos were the reason why my dad moved out of the house for months at a time."

Mac winced.

"He betrayed my mother with so many women," Rory continued. "I've always felt—and I know Shay does too—that he betrayed us, his family. He cheated on my mom and he cheated us of his time and his love, of being home when we needed him. He always put these other women before us, before me. Yet my mother took him back, still takes him back."

Okay, now a lot of Shay's crazy behavior made sense. "Hell, baby."

"He said one thing but his actions taught me the opposite."

"What do you mean?"

Rory shrugged. "He'd tell me that he was going on a work trip but a friend would tell me that she saw him at the mall with another woman. Or he'd say that he was going hunting or fishing but he never shot a damn thing. Or ever caught a fish.

"And my mother's misery was a pretty big clue that he was a-huntin' and a-fishin' for something outside the animal kingdom."

Underneath the bitterness he heard sadness and the echo of a little girl who'd lost her innocence at far too young an age.

"I thought the world of him, loved him dearly and a part of me still does. But the grown-up me doesn't like him much and, after a lifetime of lies, I can't believe a word he says. I question everything he does. As a result, trust is a difficult concept for me and has always been in short supply." Rory dredged up a smile.

Mac swallowed his rage and stopped himself from voicing his opinion about her father. Telling Rory that he thought her father was a waste of skin wouldn't make her feel better. Rory was bright and loving and giving and her father's selfishness had caused her to shrink in on herself, to limit herself to standing on the outside of love and life, looking in. She deserved to be loved and cherished and protected—by someone, not by Mac but by someone who would make her happy.

God, he wanted to thump the man for ripping that away from her.

"Tell me about your childhood, Mac," Rory softly asked, dropping her head to rest it against the back of the couch. "Dear God, that wind sounds like a banshee on crack."

"Ignore it. We're safe," Mac told her, slipping his hand between her knees. He never spoke about his blue-collar upbringing in that industrial, cold town at the back end of the world. It was firmly in his past.

But there was something about sitting in the semidark with Rory, safe from the wind and rain, that made him want to open up. "Low income, young, uneducated single mother. She had few of her own resources, either financial or emotional. She relied on a steady stream of men to provide both."

He waited to see disgust on Rory's face or, worse, pity. There was neither, she just looked at him and waited. Her lack of reaction gave him the courage to continue. "I was encouraged *not* to go to school, *not* to go to practice, not to aim for anything higher than a dead-end job at the canning factory or on one of the fishing boats. When I achieved anything, I was punished. And badly."

Rory sat up, and in the faint glow of the lamp, he could see her horrified expression. "What?"

Mac shrugged. "Crabs in a bucket."

"What are you talking about?" Rory demanded.

"You put a bunch of crabs in a bucket, one will try to climb out. The other crabs won't let that happen. They pull at the crab who's trying to escape until he falls back down. My mother was the perfect example of crab mentality. She refused to allow me to achieve anything more than what she achieved, which was pretty much nothing."

"How did you escape?"

"Stubbornness and orneriness…and my skill with a stick. I waited her out and as soon as I finished school I left. I simply refused to live her life. There was only one person in life I could rely on and that was myself. I was the only one who could make my dreams come true…"

"And you did."

Mac looked at her. Yeah, he had. The wind emitted a high, sustained shriek and Rory grabbed his hand and squeezed. He couldn't blame her; it sounded like a woman screaming for her life, and the house responded with creaks and groans.

Through the screaming wind he heard the thump of something large and he looked into the impenetrable darkness to see what had landed on the veranda. A tree branch? A plastic chair his guys had left behind? Maybe it wasn't such a good idea to stay in the living room next to the floor-to-ceiling windows, even though they were covered with boards. He stood up and hauled Rory to her feet.

It was also the perfect time to end this conversation… Looking back changed nothing and there was nothing there he wanted to remember.

"Where are we going?" she asked as he picked up the lamp.

"Bathroom."

"Why?"

"It's enclosed and probably the safest place to wait out the storm," Mac said, pulling her down the passage.

"Are we in danger?" Rory squeaked, gripping his uninjured biceps with both hands as they walked into the solidly dark house.

"No." At least, he didn't think so, but while he was prepared to take his chances with the storm, he wasn't prepared to risk Rory. Mac pulled a heavy comforter from the top shelf in the walk-in closet and handed Rory the pillows from the bed. In the bathroom, Rory helped him put a makeshift bed between the bathtub and the sink. He sat with his back to the tiled wall and Rory lay down, her head on his thigh. Touching her hair, he listened to the sounds of the storm.

Rory yawned and tipped her head back to look at him. "I'm so tired."

Mac touched her cheek with the tips of his fingers. "Go to sleep…if you can."

"Can I put my head on your shoulder?" Rory asked. "At least then, if the roof blows off, I'll have you to hold on to."

"The roof isn't going to lift, oh, dramatic one." But he shifted down, placed a pillow beneath his head and wrapped his good arm around her slim back when she placed her head on his shoulder. Her leg draped over his and her knee was achingly close to his happy place. It would be so easy, a touch here, a stroke there…

Mac kissed her forehead and pulled her closer to him. "Go to sleep, Rorks. You're safe with me."

"Tonight's conversation didn't seem that light and fluffy, Mac," Rory murmured in a sleepy voice.

It hadn't been, Mac admitted. They'd have to watch out for that. It was his last thought before exhaustion claimed him.

Eight

There was nothing like the aftermath of a hurricane to decimate a romantic atmosphere, Rory thought, standing on the debris-filled veranda and looking out toward the devastated cove. The sea had settled and broken tree branches covered the beach. A kayak had landed in the pool and there were broken chairs on the beach path. The fence surrounding the property was bent and buckled and the power lines sagged.

Mac had gone to town at first light to call someone about cleaning up the property and to check on how the small fishing village north of the cove had fared. Rory's cell phone wasn't working and she felt cut off from the world. Taking a sip from her bottle of water, she felt sweat roll down her back. It was barely 7:00 a.m. but it was very hot and horribly humid.

The scope of the damage was awful but Rory was glad

to have some time to herself, away from Mac. Yesterday had been a watershed day—the sex was explosively wonderful and the storm had scared her into opening up to Mac, and that frightened her more than the wind.

Why had she shared her past with him? She never did that! Had she been that seduced by their wonderful lovemaking? Was it the romantic atmosphere and him being all protective that prompted her to emotionally erupt? They'd agreed to keep it light but last night's conversation had been anything but! Deep and soulful conversations led to thoughts of permanence and commitment, and they'd agreed they weren't going there. She was an emotional scaredy-cat and he was incapable of commitment.

Mac, she reminded herself, didn't want a relationship anymore than she did. He'd taught himself to be his own champion and she admired the hell out of him. But he didn't need her. Anyone who could fight his way out of the enveloping negativity of Mac's childhood didn't need anyone. He'd learned to survive and then to flourish. He was emotionally self-sufficient, and a woman would never be more than an accessory and a convenience to him.

What did it matter, anyway? Rory gripped the plastic bottle so hard that it buckled in her hand, the water overflowing to trickle onto her wrist. Men always disappointed and love never lasted and the fairy tales the world fed women about happily-ever-afters were a load of hooey. No, she'd stay emotionally detached, and by doing that, she'd never feel hurt or as out of control as she had when she was a child.

Rory straightened her spine. Mac was a nice guy, a sexy guy, but he wasn't *her* guy. It would be sensible for her to remember that because if she didn't and she did something imbecilic, like fall in love with him, she was just asking for big, messy trouble.

Maybe she should stop sleeping with him...

But look at him, Rory thought, watching as Mac walked up the path from the beach. How was she supposed to resist? He was shirtless and wearing a ball cap and board shorts, his chest glistening with perspiration.

Rory leaned on the railing, and as if he sensed her watching him, he turned and looked up at her, pulling his sunglasses from his face. "Hey. You okay?"

"Fine," Rory replied. "Was the village damaged?"

"Not too bad. Trees, some missing tiles...it could've been worse. Is the power back on?"

Rory shook her head. "No. And it's so damn hot. I'm desperate for a shower."

Mac gestured to the sea behind him. "Big bathtub on our doorstep. Come on down, we'll have a swim."

Rory pulled her sticky shirt off her body. "Good idea. Do you want some water?"

Mac nodded. "And a couple of energy bars. I'm starving."

"Five minutes," Rory replied. Instead of heading inside she just stared down at him, unable to get her feet to move.

It would be so easy to love him, she thought. She was already halfway there.

Yeah, but she couldn't trust him. And what was love without trust? An empty shell that would shatter at the first knock.

Don't be stupid, Rory, she thought as she turned away. *Just don't.*

By sundown there was still no power. They gathered up a beach blanket, a lamp and a makeshift supper and headed for the beach. In the golden rays of the sunset, they cleared sticks and leaves from a patch of sand, spread out the blanket and looked at the docile sea and the sky free of all but a few small clouds.

"If it wasn't for the mess you'd think nothing had happened," Mac said, echoing her thoughts. It was scary how often he did that. Scary and a little nice.

"Fickle nature," Rory agreed, pulling her tank top over her head and dropping the shirt to the sand. She shimmied out of her shorts and stood in her plain black bikini, desperate to feel the water against her skin. She turned to Mac and found him looking at her with a strange expression on his face. "Are you okay?"

"Yeah…just thinking how gorgeous you look."

Rory flushed and lifted her hand in dismissal. "I'm already sleeping with you, McCaskill, there's no need to go overboard."

Rory turned away and walked toward the sea, foolishly hurt by his compliment. She wasn't stupid. She'd seen the pictures of him in the papers, normally accompanied by a skinny, long-legged giraffe who could grace any catwalk anywhere in the world. Shay had been his first supermodel-gorgeous girlfriend, and every girlfriend since had been slinky and sexy. Tall, dammit.

Mac's hand on her shoulder spun her around. She swallowed when she saw the irritation in his eyes. "Don't do that!"

She widened her eyes to look innocent. "Do what?"

"Dismiss me. I never say things I don't mean and if I say you look gorgeous then I mean to say that you look freakin' amazing and I can't wait to get my hands on you."

Warmth blossomed in her stomach at his backhanded compliment. Freaking amazing? Did he really think so?

"I see doubt on your face again." Mac cradled her cheek in his hand. "Why?"

Oh, jeez, he would think she was stupidly insecure and horribly lacking in confidence. Which she was, but she didn't want him to *know* that. "Uh—"

"Why, Rory?"

Rory kicked her bare foot into the sand. "Um, maybe because all the girls you normally…uh, date…are about a hundred feet tall and stacked and I'm a munchkin with a flat chest and a complex."

Mac stared at her before releasing a long, rolling laugh. Rory narrowed her eyes at him while he tried to control himself, wiping at the tears in his eyes.

"Glad I amuse you," she said, her tone frosty.

"Oh, you really do." Mac took her hand and pulled her to the sea. Thoroughly irritated with him she yanked her hand from his and dived into an oncoming wave. She started to swim, only to be jerked back by a hand on her ankle. She rolled onto her back and scowled as she tried to pull her ankle from Mac's grip.

"Let me go." She tried, unsuccessfully, to kick him.

"Pipe down…*shrimp.*"

Oh, that was fighting talk. She swiped her arm down and sprayed a stream of water into his face. Mac dropped her ankle and she launched herself at him, throwing a punch at his uninjured arm. "You jerk!"

Mac easily captured both her wrists in one hand and held them behind her back. Then he inched up two fingers to pull the strings that held her bikini top closed. He let her wrists go so he could pull the triangles over her head and toss the top onto the sand behind them before stepping back to look down at her breasts.

Moving them back into the shallows until they were standing in ankle deep water Mac placed his hands on her hips, keeping an arm's length between them. His gaze traveled from the tips of her head to where her feet disappeared into the water. Rory bit her lip and looked at the beach behind him, but Mac's fingers on her chin brought her eyes back to his face.

"I refuse to let you spend one more second thinking you are second-rate." Mac's voice was low and imbued with honesty. His fingers drifted down her neck, across her collarbone and down the swell of her breast. His thumb rubbed across her nipple and it puckered under his touch. "Yeah, you're small but perfect. So responsive, so sweet."

He bent his head and sucked her nipple into his mouth, causing her to whimper and arch her back. He licked and nibbled and then moved on to the other breast before sinking to his knees, his hands on her hips. He looked up at her, the gold and oranges of the sunset in his hair and on his face. "You are small but perfect."

He repeated the words, his thumbs tunneling under the sides of her bikini bottoms. "I lose myself in your eyes, drown in your laugh and feel at peace in your arms." His thumb skimmed over her sex and she whimpered when he touched her sweet spot. "I find myself when I'm deep inside you."

"Mac." She whimpered, needing him to…to…do something. More. Touch her, taste her. Complete her.

Rory thought she heard Mac say something like, "You are the fulfillment of every fantasy I've ever had," but all her attention was focused on his fingers, now deep inside her. He could've been proposing and she wouldn't have cared as her bikini bottoms dropped to the sand and his hot, hot mouth enveloped her.

He licked and she screamed. He repeated the motion and her knees buckled. He sucked and she fell apart, her orgasm hot and spectacular. When she sank to her knees in front of him, he tipped her flushed face upward and dropped a hot, openmouthed kiss on her lips. "As I said, you are utterly perfect. Let's swim naked," he suggested, picking up her bikini bottoms and throwing them in the same direction as her top.

Impossible man, Rory thought when her brain cells started firing again. Sexy, crazy, *impossible* man.

In the same restaurant they'd visited two weeks ago— a pink-and-yellow sunset tonight and no hurricane on the way—Mac tucked his credit card back into his wallet and gave Rory a crooked grin. "Eaten enough?"

Rory leaned back and patted her stomach. "Sorry, I'm a real girl who eats real food." *Not like those models you normally date*, she silently added.

"You ate fish stew, two empanadas and you still had pumpkin pudding." Mac shook his head. "I know every slim inch of you and I have no idea where all that food goes."

Rory picked up her drink, put the vividly green straw between her lips and sucked up some piña colada. Instead of responding, she fluttered her eyebrows at Mac, who smiled. God, she loved it when he smiled. It made her heart smile every single time.

Mac stood up and held out his hand. Rory put her hand in his and allowed him to pull her up from her chair. "Oof. You weigh a ton."

Rory slapped his shoulder. "Jerk."

"Well, you're going to work that food off."

Oh, she couldn't wait. Making love with Mac was fun, fantastic, toe-curling and, yes, it was athletic. Win win.

"What I have in mind is a bit more adventurous… Are you game?"

"Maybe," Rory carefully replied, doubt in her voice. "If it's not too kinky or too weird…"

His laughter, spontaneous and deep, rumbled across her skin and she shivered. Mac had a great laugh and, like smiling, he definitely didn't do enough of it.

"It's a surprise. A surprise that you have to work for but I promise it will be amazing." Mac brushed his lips across the top of her head. Then his arm snaked around her waist and he kissed her properly, crazily, tongues going wild. She melted against him, into him, swept up in her desire for him.

As usual, Mac was the first to pull back. He jerked back, looked down the beach and back to her mouth.

"What?" Rory pushed her hair off her face.

"Deciding whether to scrap my plans and hurry you home." Rory huffed her frustration when he stepped back and distanced himself from her. "Nope, I really want you to see this."

Mac glanced at the sunset, then at his watch and Rory noticed it was nearly dark. "Okay, it's dark enough, let's go."

"Go where?" Rory asked as he took her hand and led her down the restaurant steps toward the beach. She kicked off her sandals and sighed when her feet dipped into the still-warm sand. She picked up her shoes, slid her hand back into Mac's and followed his leisurely pace down the beach. What was he up to? And really, did it matter? It was a stunning summer's evening on the island, the air was perfumed and Mac was holding her hand, occasionally looking at her with the promise of passion in his eyes…

They walked in silence for another five minutes and then Mac angled right, walking toward the ocean until they saw a kayak and a young, hot surfer guy holding life jackets over his arm. Mac called a greeting and Surfer Boy grinned. Rory felt like a spare wheel when he bounded over the sand to pump Mac's hand, ask him how his arm was, to thank him for some tickets Mac had procured for him. Surfer Boy was about to launch into a play-by-play description when Mac interrupted him. "Marty, this is Rory. Are we all set to go?"

Marty realized he'd all but ignored her and blushed. "Sorry, hi, I didn't mean to be rude." He smiled ruefully. "I'm hockey obsessed, as you can tell. My folks have a place here so I spend my time between Vancouver and the island and I'm a huge Mavericks fan."

Rory's lips twitched in amusement. "Hi." She looked past him to the kayak at the water's edge before lifting an eyebrow in Mac's direction. "Are we're going paddling? At night?"

Mac grinned. "Yep."

"Sorry to point out the obvious, but we're not going to see much because it's dark," Rory responded. "And you definitely can't paddle with that arm."

Mac scowled. "I know and I hate it. But that's why you're paddling and I'm riding shotgun."

Rory looked at him, tall and built and strong. "Uh, Mac? I'm half your size."

"It's as flat as a mirror and it's not far. You'll be fine."

"Okay…but why?"

Mac took her hand, lifted it to his mouth and placed a hot, openedmouthed kiss on her knuckles. It was an old-fashioned, sexy gesture and Rory felt her womb quiver. "Trust me," he murmured, his eyes as deep a blue and as mysterious as the ocean beyond them. "It'll be worth it."

It was an intense moment, and Rory heard that sensible voice in her head. *Whatever is between us is about sex, not romance. Don't fall for it. Don't expect hearts and flowers along with the heat. Disappointment always follows expectations.*

She wouldn't be seduced by the island and the sunset and the heat in Mac's eyes. She would take this minute by minute, experience by experience, and she was not going to ruin it by letting her mind be seduced along with her body.

"Earth to Rory…?"

Rory saw Mac looking at her quizzically, waiting for a reply. What had he said?

"There are one or two other things I could think of that I'd rather do in the dark—" she gave Mac a mischievous look "—but what the hell. Okay."

The corners of Mac's lips kicked up and a laugh rumbled in the back of his throat.

"Funny girl," he replied in his coated-with-sin voice as Marty pretended to ignore their banter. Dropping her hand, Mac took a step back and gestured to Marty. "Right. You'll be here when we get back?"

"I'll be here," Marty promised. "You need life jackets but put on bug repellent first. And lots of it."

Marty pulled out a container from his back pocket and handed it to Rory. "If you don't slap it on everywhere, the mosquitoes will carry you away."

Rory wrinkled her nose. Where on earth were they

going? Knowing she would just have to wait and see, she rubbed the cream on her face, over her arms and down her legs. Then she pulled on a life jacket, tightened the clasps and went over to the double kayak.

She kicked off her shoes and pushed the kayak into the water before hopping into the seat. While she waited for Mac to get ready, she pulled her hair back from her face and secured it into a ponytail with the band she'd found in the back pocket of her cotton shorts. The stars were magnificent, she thought, a trillion fairy lights starting at the horizon and continuing ad infinitum.

She trailed her hand through the warm water, now impatient to get wherever they were going. Mac took the front seat after helping Marty push the kayak into deeper water, still looking irritated that he wasn't paddling— the man hated relinquishing control. Within a couple of strokes Rory found her rhythm and she followed Mac's directions across the small fisherman's harbor to what seemed to be an entrance to a coastal reserve. Mac unerringly directed her toward a channel between huge mangrove trees. Only the light of his strong flashlight penetrated the darkness. It really was an easy paddle despite Mac's bulk. She listened to the sounds coming from deep within the forest, birds and frogs, she presumed, as she navigated the low-hanging branches of a tree.

"Not far now." Mac's deep voice drifted past her ear as they leaned backward to skim under another branch. "Are you okay?"

"Sure."

"Not scared?"

"Please." She snorted her disdain. "I survived a life-threatening hurricane. Though I wouldn't mind if I was the one lounging around while you did the work."

"I wish I was. I feel like I've surrendered my man card," Mac grumbled, but she heard the grin in his voice.

"I'll reinstate it later," Rory replied in her sultriest voice.

Mac laughed and she cursed as the bow of her kayak bounced off another branch. "Dammit. How far do we have left?"

"We're almost there," Mac replied as she moved backward and around the branch with the aid of the flashlight Mac held. Rory paddled for a minute more and then the channel opened and they entered a small bay. Mac told her to head for the middle of the bay.

When she stopped, she looked at the shadows of the mangrove forest that surrounded them. The moon hung heavy in the sky and the air caressed her skin. Gorgeous.

"Look at your oar, babe," Mac softly told her. Rory glanced down and gasped with delight. Every paddle stroke left a starburst in the water, a bright streak of bioluminescence that was breathtakingly beautiful.

"Oh, my God," Rory said, pulling her hand through the water, hoping to catch a star. "That's amazing. What is it?"

"Dinoflagellates," Mac replied. "Prehistoric one-celled organisms, half animal, half plant. When they are disturbed, they respond by glowing like fireflies."

"They are marvelous. So incredibly beautiful."

"Worth the effort?" Mac asked, lazily turning around to look at her.

Rory leaned forward to rest her temple on his shoulder. "So worth it. Thank you." A fish approached the kayak and darted underneath, leaving a blue streak to mark his route.

Mac reached for her hand. Their fingers linked but

cupped, they lowered them into the water. When they lifted them out it looked like they held sparkling glitter. The water dropped back into the lagoon, and when the initial glow subsided, the glitter still danced in the water.

"The mangroves feed the organisms, releasing vitamin B12 into the water. This, with sunlight, keeps them alive," Mac told her.

Her heart thumped erratically, her fingers, in his, trembled. With want. And need. With the sheer delight of being utterly alone with him in this bay, playing in Mother Nature's jewelry box. She wanted more experiences like this with Mac. She wanted to experience the big and small of life with him. The big, like seeing the bay sparkle, the small, like sharing a Sunday-morning cup of coffee.

She wanted more than she should. She wanted it all.

Rory dipped her paddle into the water and looked at the sparkling outline...spectacular. She knew Mac was watching her profile, his gaze all coiled grace and ferocious intent.

This was beautiful. He was beautiful, too, Rory thought. But like the bioluminescent streaks, he was fleeting.

She could enjoy him, marvel over him, admire him, but he was so very, very temporary.

Nine

There was too much resistance in his arm, Rory thought, frowning. On day twenty-one of physio, a month after his injury she stood behind Mac, gently massaging his bicep and trying to figure out why he was having a buildup of lactic acid in his muscle. The resistance exercises she'd given him shouldn't have made this much of an impact. She'd been very careful to keep the exercises low-key, making sure the muscle wasn't stressed more than it needed to be.

Unless…she stiffened as a thought slapped her. Hell, no, he couldn't be that stupid, could he?

Rory held his arm, her hand perfectly still as she turned that thought over in her mind. He wouldn't be sneaky enough to go behind her back and push himself, would he?

Oh, yeah, he would.

"Problem?" Mac tipped his head back and she looked into those gorgeous, inky eyes. Look at him, all innocent. Rory whipped around the bed and stood next to him, her hands gripping her hips and her mouth tight with anger.

"Did you really think I wouldn't notice?" she demanded, making an effort to keep her anger in control.

Mac sat up slowly, and she saw he was deciding whether to bluff his way out of the situation. It would be interesting to see which way he swung, Rory thought. Would he be a grown-up and come clean, or would he act like he had no idea what she was talking about?

"I knew that I could push a little harder," Mac replied in a cool, even tone.

Points to him that he didn't try to duck the subject. Or lie.

"Did you get a physiotherapy degree in the last month or so, smarty-pants?"

Mac ignored her sarcasm. "I know my body, Rory. I know what I can handle."

"And I have a master's degree in physiotherapy specializing in sports injuries, you moron! I know what can go wrong if you push too hard too fast!" Rory yelled, deeply angry. "Are you so arrogant you think you know better than I do? That my degrees mean nothing because you know your body?"

"I utterly respect what you do," Mac calmly stated, linking his hands on his stomach, "but you don't seem to understand that this body is my tool, my machine. I know it inside out and I need you to trust me to know how far I can push myself."

"You *need* to *trust* me to know what's best for you in this situation," Rory shouted. "This is a career-threatening injury, Mac!"

"I know that!" Mac raised his voice as well, swinging his legs over the edge of the bed. "Do you not think I don't lie awake every night wondering if I'm going to regain full movement, whether I'll be able to compete again? The scenarios run over and over in my head, but I've got to keep moving forward. That means working it."

"That means resting it," Rory retorted. "You're pushing too hard."

"You're not pushing me enough!" Mac yelled as he stood up. "I can do this, Rory."

Rory looked at him and shook her head. *Look at him, all muscle and hardheadedness*, she thought. Beautiful but so incredibly flawed. He had to go full tilt, had to push the envelope. But he refused to accept that this envelope was made of tissue paper and could rip at a moment's notice.

Would rip at a moment's notice.

She couldn't stop him, she realized. He'd ignore her advice and go his own way.

Rory lifted her hands, palms out. "I can't talk to you right now."

"Rorks—"

"I'm not discussing this right now." Rory walked toward the door.

Mac's arm shot out to block her way. When she tried to duck underneath it, he wrapped his arm around her waist and held her, far too easily, against his chest. "No, you're not just walking out. We're going to finish this argument. We're adults. That's what adults do."

"Let me go, Mac." Rory pushed against his arm. She struggled against him, desperate to get away.

"God, you smell so good." Mac dropped his mouth to her shoulder and nuzzled her. His teeth scraped over her skin and Rory shuddered, feeling heat pool low in her abdomen. She shouldn't be doing this, she thought. She should be walking away, but Mac's hand cupping her breast, his thumb gliding over her nipple, shoved that thought away.

Stupid, stupid, stupid, she thought as she arched her back and pushed her breast into his palm. Mac pulled her nipple through the cotton fabric as he pushed the straps of her shirt and bra down her shoulder with his teeth. His breath was warm on her skin and she reached back to place her hand on the hair-roughened skin of his thigh, just below the edge of his shorts. Hard muscle tensed beneath her hand and he groaned as he pushed his erection into her lower back.

Ooh, nice. Rory twisted her head up and back, and Mac met her lips with his, his tongue invading her mouth to tangle lazily with hers. Damn, he kissed like a dream. His kisses could charm birds from trees, move mountains, persuade a nun to drop her habit...

Persuade. The word lodged in her head and she couldn't jog it loose. She tensed in his arms as she pulled her head away from his. Persuade. Coax. Cajole.

Seduce.

Rory closed her eyes and slumped against him. God, she was such a sap, so damn stupid. Mac was distracting her from the argument, hoping she'd forget he'd gone behind her back. He used her attraction to him against her, thinking that if he gave her a good time, she'd forgive him for being a colossal jerk!

She pushed his arm and stumbled away from him, shoving her hair from her face with both hands. God, she finally understood how being in a man's arms could make you go against your principles.

This is how it would be with him; she'd object, he'd seduce her into changing her mind. I get it, Mom, I do. But unlike you, I'm going to listen to my head and not my hormones.

Rory locked her knees to keep herself upright and took a deep breath, looking for control. She pulled down the hem of her T-shirt, wishing she were in her tunic and track pants, her uniform. She'd feel far more in control, professional.

"Did you really think I'd fall for your little let's-seduce-her-to-get-me-out-of-trouble routine? I'm not that shallow or that stupid. And you're not that good." Rory slapped her fists on her hips, ignoring the flash of angry surprise she saw in his eyes. "You went behind my back to exercise your arm. That was devious and manipulative. I don't like dishonesty, Mac, in any form. Because of that and because you obviously don't trust me, I think it's best that I leave."

She could see from the expression on his face that he thought she was overreacting. Maybe she was, but he'd given her the perfect excuse to run. To get out of this quicksand relationship before she was in over her head and unable to leave.

"Our contract will become null and void," Mac said, his voice devoid of anger or any emotion at all.

"I don't care." Rory told him. She wanted her clinic, but not at the cost of living in quicksand. "I'm going upstairs to pack. I'll be out of your hair in a couple of hours."

Mac swore and swiped his hand across his face. "God, Rory…running away is not the solution!"

"No, the solution is you being honest with me, listening to me, but you won't do that, so we have nothing to talk about," Rory snapped before walking out the door. Yes, she was scared, but she couldn't forget that he'd been dishonest with her. That was unacceptable.

She'd forgotten, she thought as she ran up the stairs to her room. *You can't trust him; you can't trust anyone. Disappointment comes easily to those who expect too much. Don't expect. Don't trust.*

She wouldn't do it again. She wouldn't be that much of a fool. Mac would do his own thing, always had and always would. It was how he operated. He'd charm with his sincerity, his kisses. He'd say all the right things but nothing would change, not really.

The best predictor of future behavior was past behavior, she reminded herself.

"I'm sorry I went behind your back, but I was trying to avoid an argument," Mac said from the doorway to her bedroom.

"Well, you got one anyway." Rory picked up a pile of T-shirts and carefully placed them in her suitcase, her back to him.

Mac leaned his shoulder into the door frame and felt like he'd been catapulted back ten years. The argument was different but her method of dealing with conflict was exactly the same as her sister's.

The difference between the two sisters was that he *wanted* to apologize to Rory, *needed* to sort this out. He didn't want her to run.

"I didn't touch you to distract you or to get out of trouble. You're right, I'm not that good."

Rory's narrowed eyes told him he had a way to go before he dug himself out of this hole. But that particular point was an argument for another day. He sighed. "And yes, I should've been upfront with you about doing the exercises. Though, in my defense, it's been a very long time since I asked anybody for permission to do anything."

Like, never.

"The lie bothers me, but it's the insult to my intelligence that I find truly offensive. That you would think I wouldn't realize…"

Ouch. Mac winced. "Yeah, I get that."

Rory sighed. "That being said, I can't take lies, Mac. Or evasions or half-truths."

Rory tossed a pair of flip-flops onto the pile of shirts in her suitcase. Mac cursed himself for being an idiot. She'd told him about her father and his deceit, and if he'd thought about it, he would've realized keeping secrets from her was a very bad idea.

He sucked at relationships and that was why he avoided them. So if he was avoiding relationships, why the hell was he determined to get her to stay?

"Don't go, Rorks. It isn't necessary. I need you. I can't do this without you."

He could, but he didn't want to. A subtle but stunning difference.

He needed her. For something other than her skill as a physio and the way she made him feel in bed. It was more than that…his need for her went beyond the surface of sex and skill.

Dammit, he hated the concept of needing anyone for anything. It made him feel…weak. He was a grown man who'd worked damn hard to make sure he never felt that way again.

Yet he was prepared to beg if he had to. "Please? Stay."

Rory turned slowly. "Will you listen to me?"

"I'll try," he conceded, and lifted his hand at her

frown. He wasn't about to make promises he couldn't keep, not even for her. "Will you try to accept that I know my body, know what I can do with it?"

"It's such a huge risk, Mac." Rory bit her lip. "You're playing Russian roulette and you might not win."

"But what if I do?" Mac replied. "If I do, I place myself and my team and my friends in a lot stronger position than we are currently in. It's a risk I'm willing to take."

"I'm not sure that I am." Rory sat down on the edge of the bed. "I have a professional responsibility to do what's best for you, and this isn't it."

"I'll sign any waiver you want me to," Mac quickly said.

Rory waved his offer away. "It's more than playing a game of covering the legalities, McCaskill. This is your career, your livelihood at stake."

"But it's *my* career, *my* livelihood." Mac held her eye. "My decision, Rory, and I'm asking you this *one time* to trust me. I can't live with negativity, I just can't."

"I'm not being negative, I'm being realistic," Rory retorted.

"Your perception of reality isn't mine." Mac sat down next to her on the bed and looked down at the cotton rug below his feet. "I really believe that part of the reason why I've been successful at what I try is that I don't entertain negativity. At all. If I can think it, I can do it, and I don't allow doubt. I need you to think the same."

"Look, I believe in the power of the mind, but everything I've ever been taught tells me you need time, you need to nurse this… It will be a miracle if you regain full strength in that arm."

He couldn't force her to believe, Mac thought in frustration. He wished he could. He blew air into his cheeks and rolled his head to release the tension in his neck.

"Okay. But if you can't be positive then I need you to be quiet." She started to blast him with a retort but he spoke over her. "I'm asking you—on bended knee if I must—to stay and to trust me when I tell you that I know my body. I won't push myself beyond what I can do." Here came the compromise. It sucked but he knew he didn't have a chance of her staying without it. "I won't do anything behind your back and I will listen, and respect, your opinion. I still need your help, if only to keep my crazy in check."

Rory stared at the floor, considering his words, and he knew she was wavering.

"You told me about your clinic, how much having your own place means to you. Don't give up on your dreams for your own practice because I'm a stubborn ass who doesn't know the meaning of the word *quit*."

Rory lifted her head to glare at him. "Low blow, Mc-Caskill, using my dreams to get me to do what you want me to do."

He shrugged as Rory glared at him. He didn't want her to leave and he would use any method he could to keep her on this island with him. He was that desperate.

"So, you'll stay?"

"For now." She pointed a finger at him. "You dodged a bullet, Mac. Don't make me shoot you for real next time."

On the private jet hired for the trip home, Rory watched as Mac stashed his laptop back in a storage space above his head. Looking at him, no one would realize Mac had gone through major surgery nearly eight weeks ago. She listened to him bantering with the flight attendant and couldn't help wondering if Mac was doing exercises on the side, working that arm in ways she didn't approve of.

Maybe. Possibly. His recovery was remarkable.

Rory thought back to their argument, still a little angry that he'd deceived her. Maybe it wasn't deliberate, maybe he'd just been thoughtless, but it had hurt. On the positive side, the argument had opened her eyes. It had been her wake-up call. From that moment on she'd stopped entertaining, even on the smallest scale, thoughts about a happy-ever-after with Mac.

He'd never be a hundred percent honest with her and she could never fully trust him.

There couldn't be love or any type of a relationship without trust, and she had to be able to trust a man with everything she had. She couldn't trust Mac so she couldn't love him. She'd decided that…hadn't she?

Okay, it was a work in progress.

The flight attendant moved away and Mac stretched out his legs, looking past Rory out the window by her head. Below them the island of Puerto Rico was a verdant dot in an aqua sea and their magical time together was over.

Back to reality.

Mac sipped his beer and placed his ankle on his knee. "This plane can't fly fast enough. Kade sounded stressed."

"He didn't say why he wanted you back in the city?" Rory asked. Mac had announced at breakfast that Kade needed him in Vancouver and by mid-morning they were on their way home.

Mac shook his head. "No, and that worries me." A frown pulled his eyebrows together and his eyes were bleak. He looked down at his injured arm and traced the red scar that was a memento of his operation. "What if it doesn't heal correctly? What will I do?"

She'd never heard that note in his voice before—part fear, part insecurity. "You go to plan B, Mac. There is always another plan to be made, isn't there?"

Mac picked up her hand and wound his fingers in hers. "But hockey is what I do, who I am. It's my dream, my destiny, the reason I get up in the morning."

Is that what he really thought? She stared down at his long, lean body. It was a revelation to realize she wasn't the only one in this plane with demons. She felt relieved, and sad, at the thought. "Yeah, you're a great hockey player, supposedly one of the best."

Mac mock-glared at her and she smiled. "Okay, you *are* the best…does that satisfy your monstrous ego?"

Mac's lips twitched but he lowered his face so she couldn't look into his eyes. That was okay. It would be easier to say this without the distraction of his fabulous eyes. "You aren't what you do, Mac. You're so much more than that."

"I play hockey, Rory, that's it."

Rory shook her head in disagreement. "You are an amazing businessperson, someone who has many business interests besides hockey. You are a spokesperson for various charities, you play golf and you do triathlons in the off-season. Hockey is not who you are or all that you do."

"But it's what I love best and if I can't do it…if I can't save the team by keeping it out of Chenko's clutches, I will have failed. It would be the biggest failure of my life." Mac sat up, pulled his hand from hers and gripped the armrests. *"I don't like to fail."*

"None of us do, Mac. You're not alone in that," Rory responded, her voice tart. "So, the future of the Mavericks is all resting on your shoulders? Kade and Quinn have no part to play?"

"Yes—no… I'm the one who was injured," Mac protested.

"Here's a news flash, dude, hockey players get hurt. They sustain injuries all the time. Kade and Quinn, if I remember correctly, are both out of the game because of their injuries. You getting injured was just a matter of time. You couldn't keep ducking that bullet forever! It's part of the deal and you can't whine about it."

"I am not whining!" Mac protested, his eyes hot.

Rory smiled. "Okay, you weren't whining. But your thinking is flawed. You are not a superhero and you are not invincible and you are not solely responsible for the future of the Mavericks. If you can't play again, you will find something else to do, and I have no doubt you will be successful at it. You are not a crab and there is no bucket."

Mac stared at her for a long time and eventually the smallest smile touched his lips, his eyes. He released a long sigh and sent her a frustrated look. "You might be perfectly gorgeous but you are also a perfect pain in my ass. Especially when you're being wise."

The mischievous grin that followed his words suggested their heart-to-heart was over. "Want to join the Mile High Club?"

Rory grinned. "What's that word I'm looking for? No? *No* would be it."

Mac turned in his seat and nuzzled her neck with his lips. "Bet I could change your mind."

"You're good, but not that good, McCaskill." Rory

tipped her head to allow him to kiss that sensitive spot under her ear. "But you're welcome to try."

Note to self: Mac McCaskill cannot walk away from a challenge.

Kade met them at the airport and kissed Rory's cheek before pulling Mac into that handshake/half hug they did so well. "Sorry to pull you back from the island sooner than expected, but I need you here."

Mac frowned. "What's happened?"

Kade looked around, saw that they were garnering attention and shook his head. "Not here. We'll get into it in the car. No, Rory, don't worry about your luggage, I've sent an intern to pick it up."

Nice, Rory thought. She could get used to this first-class life. She pulled her large tote bag over her shoulder, saw fans lifting their cell phones in their direction and wished she'd worn something other than a pair of faded jeans and a loose cotton shirt for the journey home. They'd both showered on the jet but Mac had changed from his cargo shorts and flip-flops into a pistachio-green jacket, a gray T-shirt and khaki pants. He looked like the celebrity he was and she looked like a backpacker.

Sigh.

Rory stepped away, distancing herself as fans approached Mac and Kade for their autographs. After signing a few, Mac jerked his head in her direction and the three of them started walking—Rory at a half jog. In the VIP parking lot, Kade finally stopped at a low silver sports car and opened the back door for Rory to slide in. Mac took the passenger seat next to Kade and within minutes they were on the highway heading back to the city.

"Talk." Mac half twisted in his seat to look at Kade, pulling his designer cap off his head and running his hand through his hair. "What's up? Why did we have to get home so quickly?"

Rory heard the note of irritation in Mac's voice. Funny, she would've thought he'd be happy to be returning home, to be getting back into the swing of things. Yet she couldn't deny they'd been enjoying the solitude of Cap de Mar, the long, lazy sun- and sea-filled days punctured by long, intense bouts of making love.

"How's your arm?" Kade replied.

"Fine."

Rory rolled her eyes. "Fine" was boy-speak for "I don't want to talk about it."

"Improving," Rory chimed in half a beat behind him. She ignored Mac's narrowed eyes and continued to speak. "It's a lot better but he's definitely not ready to play yet. If that's what you are thinking, then you can forget about it."

"I could play," Mac said, his tone resolute.

"Do it and die," Rory stated in a flat, don't-test-me voice. Hadn't they had this argument? Had he heard anything she'd said?

Kade swore, ducked around a pickup truck and a station wagon and floored the accelerator. Rory prayed they would arrive at their destination—wherever that was—in one piece.

Where was her destination? Mavericks' headquarters? Mac's house? Her apartment? She and Mac had been living together, sleeping together, for a little more than a month. But now they were back to normal and island rules didn't necessarily apply to Vancouver. Right, this was another reason why she avoided relationships; she hated walking through the minefield of what was socially acceptable.

"Slow down, bud. Not everyone craves your need for speed."

Kade slowed down from the speed of light to pretty damn fast. She'd take it, Rory decided, and loosened her hold on her seat belt.

"Right," Mac continued. "What's going on?"

Rory saw Kade's broad shoulder lift and drop, taut with tension. "God, so much. First, the press, especially the sports writers, are speculating that your injury is a lot worse than we've been admitting to and they are looking for the angles. Speculation has been running wild."

Rory saw a muscle jump in Mac's cheek and she wondered what it was like to live life under a microscope.

"Widow Hasselback is also asking how you are and I heard she met with the suits from the Chenko Corporation last week. She told me they've increased their offer."

Mac closed his eyes and gripped the bridge of his nose with his thumb and forefinger. His curse bounced around the car. "That's not all," he said.

"I wish it was," Kade agreed. "Bayliss, our new investor, would like to watch a practice match before making a commitment."

Mac frowned. "That wouldn't normally be a problem. We often have people coming to watch practice, but so many of the team are still on vacation."

"Between us, Quinn and I have reached them all. They understand what's at stake and they'll be there," Kade reassured him.

Mac pulled out his cell phone and swiped his thumb across the screen. "Scheduled for when?"

Kade's worried glance bounced off hers in the rear-view mirror. "The day after tomorrow. At four." He looked apologetic. "According to Bayliss, it's a take-it-or-leave-it deal."

The day. After. Tomorrow.

Rory shook her head. "Well, that's all fine and good but you can count Mac out of that match."

"I'm playing," Mac said, and she immediately recognized his don't-argue-with-me voice.

Well, this time she would out-stubborn him. Rory pulled in a breath and reminded herself to keep calm. Yelling at Mac would achieve nothing. If she wanted to win this argument she would have to sound reasonable and in control. And professional. "I admit that your arm is vastly improved and that no one, looking at you, would suspect how serious your injury actually is. But it's not mended, and one wrong move or twist would undo all the healing you've done and possibly, probably, aggravate the injury further."

"I'm fine, babe."

"You are not fine!" Rory heard her voice rise and she deliberately toned it down. "You are not fully recovered and you certainly don't have all your strength back. I strongly suggest, as your physiotherapist, that you sit this one out."

Mac ignored her to nod at Kade. "I'll be there."

"Did you hear anything I said?" Rory demanded from the backseat, her face flushed with anger. "Do you know what you are risking? One slap shot, one bump and that's it, career over, McCaskill!"

"Stop being dramatic, Rory," Mac said in a hard, flat voice. "I keep telling you that I know what I am capable of and you've got to trust me. I know what I'm doing."

"I know that you are being a friggin' idiot!" Rory shouted.

Mac turned around and looked her in the eye. His direct gaze locked on hers and she immediately realized that nothing she could say or do would change his mind. He was playing, nearly two months after surgery. He was risking his career, all the work they'd done… Rory felt like he was tossing away all her hard work too.

"I took my vacation time to help you heal. I've spent hours working on you, working on getting you to where you are right now. You play and you've wasted my time and your money," Rory said, her voice rising along with her anger.

"I don't have a choice, dammit! Why can't you understand that?" Mac yelled back. "This is about my family, my team, securing something that means more to me than anything else!"

Of course it did, Rory realized. To Mac, the Mavericks were everything. He wouldn't change his mind or see reason. Kade and Quinn and the team would always be his top priorities. Her opinion, as his lover or his physiotherapist, didn't really count.

She was done fighting him, done fighting this. Why did she care anyway? This was a temporary affair, a fling. He was a client. At the end of the day it was his choice whether to mess up his life or not; she had no say in it. It was his arm, his career, his future, his stupidity.

But she didn't have to be part of it. Rory sucked in air, found none and pushed the button to open her window a crack. Cool, rain-tinged air swirled around her head and she lifted her face to cool her temper. "You do this and I'm out of here. Professionally and personally."

"Are you serious?" Mac demanded, his tone hard and, maybe she was being a bit fanciful, tinged with hurt.

"Hell, Rory," Kade murmured.

"It's my professional opinion that your arm is insufficiently healed to play competitive hockey. I am not going to watch you undo all the hard work we've done and I am certainly not going to watch you injure yourself further."

Mac rubbed the back of his neck and he darted a scowl at Kade. "Pretend you're not here," he told him.

"Done," Kade promptly replied.

Mac turned his attention to her and she pushed her back into her seat, not sure what he was about to say. She just knew it would be important. "Rory, listen to me."

She dropped her gaze and closed her eyes. When he looked at her like that, all open and exposed, she found it hard to concentrate.

"No, look at me…"

Rory forced her eyes open.

"I know that asking you to trust me is difficult for you. It's not something you do easily. And I know I'm asking you to put aside your learning and your experience. You think that I believe I'm invincible or a superhero. I'm not. I know I'm not… I'm just someone who knows what he is capable of, what his body is capable of. This isn't just a practice match. It's the most important practice match of my life, of Kade's life, of Quinn's. If I sit it out I'm risking this team, my friends' futures, my brothers' futures. This isn't about me and my ego."

"It will be about you if you do more damage to your arm. Then neither you nor your team will have a future… or the future you want." Couldn't he see she was trying to protect him from himself? She was trying to be the voice of reason here?

"Trust me, Rory. Please, just this once. Trust me to know what I'm doing. Stand by me, support me. Do that by coming to the practice, make sure that my arm is taped correctly. It'll be fine. I'll be fine. Be positive."

"And if I don't?" Rory demanded.

Mac just shrugged before quietly telling her that he'd play anyway.

"So, really, this entire argument has been a waste of time." Rory turned away so he didn't see the burning tears in her eyes. With blurry vision she noticed that Kade was turning down Mac's street, and within a minute he stopped the car.

The silence was as heavy as the freighter that was making its way across the bay as Mac unclipped his seatbelt and opened his door.

"One of the interns will be along shortly with your luggage," Kade told him, giving him a fist bump. Mac gripped his shoulder and squeezed before leaving the car. In the open doorway Mac bent his knees to look over his seat at Rory. "You joining me, Rory?"

No. She wanted to go home, pull on her pajamas, grab a glass of wine and cry. "I don't think so."

Mac gave her a sharp nod and his lips tightened with annoyance. "As you wish. I'm certainly not going to beg."

"Like you would know how," Rory muttered, and his eyes flashed as he slammed the door shut on her words.

Rory folded her arms across her chest and hoped Kade didn't notice that her hands were shaking. "Can you take me home, Kade?"

"Yep. Can do. Come and sit up here with me."

Ten

Was she just being stubborn, Rory wondered as Kade capably, and silently, maneuvered his very fancy sports car through the city streets? She'd always been the type of therapist who encouraged her patients to listen to their bodies, to tune in to how they were feeling. She generally listened. If they said they felt better, she trusted they were telling the truth. Why couldn't she do that with Mac? Why was she balking?

Because there was so much at stake. This one decision could have far-reaching and potentially devastating consequences. Mac loved hockey above everything else and he was risking his entire career on a still fragile tendon and a practice match. She didn't want him to lose all that he'd worked for. He might be willing to risk it, but she wasn't prepared to sanction that risk. He was thinking of the team, she was thinking about him—only him.

There had to be another way. There was always another way. They just hadn't thought about it yet.

"Would it be such a bad idea to let this corporation buy the Mavericks?" she abruptly asked Kade.

Kade considered his response. "It would definitely be different. They have a history of clearing the deck and changing all the management, the leadership. That would mean Quinn, Mac and I would be figuratively on the streets."

"Other teams would snap you up," Rory argued.

Kade nodded as he stopped at a traffic light. "Sure, but we wouldn't be on the *same* team. We've been together for nearly fifteen years, Rory. We fight and argue and irritate each other to death but we know each other. We *trust* each other."

"There's that damn word again," Rory muttered.

"One you seem to have a problem with," Kade observed, sending her a smile. He really was a very good-looking man, Rory noticed. Not Mac hot, but still…phew!

"Am I being unreasonable?" she demanded, slapping her hand repeatedly against the dashboard. "The man has been injured! It was serious. I'm trying to protect him."

"Yeah. And he's asking you to trust him to know what he's doing," Kade responded, gently removing her hand from his dashboard and dropping it back into her lap. "It's too expensive a car to be used as a punching bag, honey."

Rory winced. "Sorry." She shoved her hands under her thighs to keep them from touching something she shouldn't and sighed heavily. "He makes me nuts."

Kade laughed. "I suspect he feels the same way about you." He tapped his finger against the steering wheel before turning his head to look at her. "Mac never asks anyone for anything."

Rory looked puzzled, not sure where he was going with this.

"He injured his arm because he tried to move a fridge on his own, something either Quinn or I or any of his teammates, coaching staff, support crew, maintenance guys or office staff would've helped him with...*had he asked*."

"Try living with him for nearly two months," Rory muttered, reminded of all the arguments she'd had with Mac. "I think it has something to do with the fact that his mother was emotionally, probably physically, neglectful of him. He learned not to ask because his needs were never met," she mused.

Kade switched lanes and sent her an astonished look. "He told you about his mother?"

"Not much. A little." Rory shrugged.

"Holy crap."

Rory shrugged again, brushing off his astonishment. "Not asking for help is stupid. Everyone needs someone at some time in their lives."

"I agree. I've been trying to tell him that for years," Kade said, turning into her street. He pulled up behind a battered pickup and switched off the growling engine. Pushing his sunglasses up into his hair, he half turned in his seat. "So, we agree that we are talking about a man who is ridiculously independent and stupidly self-sufficient and hates asking for a damn thing?"

"Precisely," Rory agreed, reaching for her bag, which sat on the floor by her feet. She dug around for her house keys and pulled out the bunch with a flourish. "Found them! Yay."

Kade's hand on her arm stopped her exit from the car. When she looked back at him, his expression was serious. "Interesting then that our self-sufficient, hate-to-ask-for-anything friend asked you to be there at the practice game, asked you to trust him. Practically begged you…"

Rory sucked in a breath and scowled at him. "Oh, you're good," she muttered as she stepped out of the car.

"So I'm frequently told," Kade smugly replied. Rory shook her head as she climbed out of the low seat, charmed and amused despite the fact that he'd backed her into a corner. She turned back to look at him and he grinned at her through her open window. "Frequently followed by…*can we do that again?*"

Rory slapped a hand across her eyes.

"I'll leave your name with security. Day after tomorrow. Four p.m."

Rory managed, using an enormous amount of self-control, not to kick his very expensive tires as he pulled away.

Mac couldn't help glancing around the empty arena as he hit the rink, as at home on the ice as he was on his own two feet. Stupid to hope that she'd be here. Intensely stupid to feel disappointed. There was nothing between them except some hot sex and a couple of conversations.

He was happy the way he was, happy to have the odd affair with a beautiful woman, happy with his lone-wolf lifestyle. Wasn't he?

Not so much.

Mac glanced at the empty seats and banged his stick on the ice in frustration. One thing. He'd asked her one damn thing and she'd refused. Talk about history repeating itself… It served him right for putting himself out there. He'd learned the lesson hard and he'd learned the lesson well that when it came to personal relationships, when he asked, he didn't always receive. With his mother he'd never received anything he needed.

His childhood was over, he reminded himself.

Besides, it didn't matter, he had an investor to impress, a team to save, Vernon's legacy to protect. Mac glanced over toward the coach's area and immediately saw Quinn and Kade standing, like two mammoth sentries, on either side of a slim woman and an elderly man who bore a vague resemblance to Yoda. The woman wore jeans and a felt hat and the older man was dressed in corduroy pants and a parka. These were their investors? Where were the suits, the heels, the briefcases?

Hope you have what we need, old man, Mac thought, as the rest of the team followed him onto the ice. Hellfire, his arm was already throbbing and he'd yet to smack a puck.

Maybe Rory was right and playing wasn't such a great idea. He swung his injured arm and only sheer force of will kept him from grimacing. The team physio had strapped his arm to give it extra support but the straps were misaligned and, he was afraid, doing more harm than good.

Crapdammithell!

"McCaskill!"

Mac spun on his skates and there she stood, a resigned look on her face. His heart bumped and settled as he skated toward her. She stood next to a large man who looked familiar, and it took Mac a minute to place him. His nurse from The Annex…what was his name? Troy? Unlike Rory, Troy was wearing a huge smile and his gaze bounced from player to player in the manner of a true fan.

Mac stopped at the boards in front of Rory and sent her a slow smile. Damn, he'd missed her.

"Thanks for coming," he said, wishing he could take her into his arms, kiss her senseless. He wanted, just for a moment, to step out of these skates, out of the arena and into the heat of her mouth, to feel her pliant, slim, sexy body beneath his hands. Huh. That had never happened before. Skating, hockey, the ice…nothing could normally top that.

Mac looked at Rory, arms folded across her chest, her expression disapproving. That didn't worry him; he'd learned to look for the emotion in her eyes. Those gray depths told him everything he needed to know about how she was feeling. Yeah, she was worried, but resigned. A little scared, but he could see that she was trying to trust him, trying to push aside her intellect to give him the benefit of the doubt.

Rory narrowed her amazing eyes at him. "I'm not for one moment condoning this, and if you do any more damage I will personally kick your ass."

Deeply moved—he understood how hard this was for her—he sent her a crooked grin, silently thanking her for taking this chance on him, on them.

Rory, stubborn as always, tried to look stern but her eyes lightened with self-deprecating humor. And, as always, there was a hint of desire. For the first time, he easily recognized tenderness in her steady gaze.

And concern. She was so damned worried about him. When last had someone cared this much? Never? Mac felt his heart thump, unaccustomed to feeling saturated with emotion.

"Noted," Mac gruffly said, needing a moment to regroup. Or ten. Pulling in a deep breath he pulled off his glove with his teeth and held out his hand for Troy to shake. "Good to see you."

Troy pumped his hand with an enthusiasm that had Mac holding back a wince. "You play?" he asked Troy.

Troy nodded. "College."

"When we're finished with the practice match, maybe you'd like to borrow some skates and join us on the ice?" Mac asked.

Troy looked delighted. "Awesome. My gear is in the car so I don't need to borrow a thing. Wow. Awe. Some."

Rory rolled her eyes and looked at Mac again. "You okay?"

"Pretty much. Better now that you are here." Mac looked over the ice to the other side of the rink, where Kade and Quinn were still in deep conversation with the investor. Quinn didn't look like he was about to call the team to order anytime soon. "Speaking of, can I borrow you for a sec?"

Rory nodded and he pushed open the hinge board and stepped off the ice. He sat on a chair and looked up at Troy. "It's great that you are so damn big, dude."

Troy grinned and made a production of fluttering his eyes at him. "I didn't think you noticed."

"Cut it out, Troy," Rory muttered.

Mac laughed and jerked his thumb toward Rory. "She's more my type. But I do need you to stand in front of me so Quinn and Kade, and especially that small old guy, can't see me."

Troy, smart guy, immediately moved into position. "Like this?"

"That works." Mac pulled off his jersey and leaned down and grabbed Rory's bag, holding it out to her. "I need you to re-tape my arm. The team physio did it but he's done something wrong, it's hurting like a bitch."

Rory looked like she was about to say "I told you so," and he appreciated her effort to swallow the words. While he ripped the stabilizing tape off his arm with his other hand, taking quite a bit of arm hair with it, Rory pulled out another roll of tape. He groaned when he saw that it was bright pink. "You're kidding me, right?"

"Consider it my silent protest," Rory said, a smile touching her mouth. She was still worried about him. He could see it in her eyes, in her tight smile. But she cut the tape into strips and carefully ran the tape over his biceps and elbow, her eyes narrowed in concentration.

"Quinn's getting ready to move," Troy told them.

"Nearly there," Rory muttered, smoothing the end of the last piece of tape across the other two. She nodded. "That should give you more support, especially when you extend."

Mac did a biceps curl and he sighed with relief. He took the jersey Rory held out to him and pulled it over his head. When he was dressed, he stood up and dropped a hot, openmouthed kiss on her lips. "You are brilliant."

"Do *not* hurt yourself."

"Don't nag." Mac kissed her again, still in awe that she was here, that she was helping him, standing by him, doing this. She'd shoved aside her training, had placed her trust in him, something she so rarely gave...

Quinn's impatient whistle broke into his thoughts and his voice drifted across the ice calling them to order. Mac turned back to Rory. "Kade has invited the team and some suits to a cocktail party tonight at Siba's. You know—the bar in the Forrester Hotel? Meet me there at seven?"

Rory scowled at him but her eyes were soft and still scared. "Maybe, if you're not back in the hospital."

Mac grinned at Troy. "Such a sarcastic little ray of sunshine. Thanks for your help. I'll see you in a bit."

"She'll be there," Troy told him.

"You'll damn well go," Mac heard Troy telling Rory as he skated, slowly it had to be said, away from them. "That man is nuts about you."

He really was, he reluctantly admitted.

"You are so in love with him," Troy crowed as he flung his hockey bag into the trunk of his battered SUV. Rory eyed his piece of rusty metal; she hated driving anywhere with Troy because she was quite certain her chances of, well, dying were increased a thousand percent whenever its tires met the road.

Rory, her hand on the passenger-door handle, looked down at the front wheel and sighed her relief. The tires had been changed and Troy had promised her it had just had its biyearly service. Rory had replied that it needed a funeral service but she'd eventually abandoned her idea of taking a taxi to the arena and allowed Troy to drive her in his chariot of death.

Rory tugged at the handle and cursed when it refused to open. Troy, already behind the wheel, reached across and thumped the panel and the door sprung open, just missing hitting Rory in the face. "I hate this car," she muttered, climbing in.

Troy nodded his head. "Yeah, me too. But it's paid for, thereby freeing up money for the nursing home."

Rory, grateful that they'd left the subject of Mac and her feelings, sent him a concerned look. "How is your mom? Any more walkabouts?"

Troy momentarily closed his eyes. "No, she's fine. Well, as fine as she can be." He stared at the luxury car parked next to them. "I've found a home just outside the city, a place that looks fantastic. They have space for her, could take her tomorrow, but I just can't afford it."

"I could…" She had to offer to loan him the money. He wouldn't take it, but she wished he would. He was her best friend, an almost-brother…why didn't he realize that she'd move mountains for him if she could?

Troy sighed. "I love you for offering but…no. I can't." Troy turned the key and the car spluttered and died. He cursed, cranked it again and Rory held her breath. It rumbled, jerked and eventually put-putted to life. "You wouldn't think that I'd just had it serviced, would you?"

"Nope. Then again, I think trying to service this car is like putting a Band-Aid on a slit throat."

"Nice," Troy said as they pulled out of the arena parking lot. "Let's get back to the interesting stuff. When did you fall in love with Mac?"

"Ten years ago," Rory replied without thinking. She jerked up and scowled at her friend. "I didn't just say that out loud, did I?"

Troy grinned. "You so did."

"Dammit." She didn't want to be in love with Mac. That meant she had to give him up, she'd have to retreat, do what she did best to protect herself and fade away. Loving Mac carried too many risks, too much potential heartache.

"So, are you going to keep Mac around or are you going to dump him when he gets too close?"

Lord, Troy knew her well. She had to make a token protest. "I don't do that."

Troy snorted. "Honey, you *always* do that. You meet a guy, you go on a couple of dates and when you think something might have a chance of developing, you find an excuse to dump him. You have massive trust issues."

"So does Mac. He also has abandonment issues!" she added.

"It's not a competition, Rory! Jeez," Troy snapped as they approached the first set of traffic lights. "Man, these brakes are soft. Didn't they check them?" They stopped and Troy looked at her. "Okay...continue."

Rory stared at the drops of rain running down the windshield. She might as well tell him, she thought, he knew everything else about her. "You know how Shay loves to tease me about stealing her boyfriends?"

"Yeah, and you get all huffy and defensive and embarrassed."

"She was dating Mac when she walked in on us...we were about to kiss," Rory quietly stated. "How would she feel if I started dating him, started a relationship with him?"

"I bet she'd be fine with it." Tory rolled his eyes, and without taking his eyes off the road instructed his cell phone to call Shay.

"What are you doing?" Rory demanded.

"Calling Shay," Troy replied, as if she were the biggest idiot in the world. Which she was, because she was talking to him about Mac.

"Troyks!" Shay's bubbly voice filled the car.

"Hey, oh gorgeous one. I'm in the car with Rory and we have a question for you."

"Shoot," Shay replied.

"It's not important—" Rory stated, leaning sideways to talk into the phone.

"Back off, sister." Troy growled. "Rory's using you as an excuse not to date Mac McCaskill. So how would you feel about them getting it on? You know, even though you're married to the hunkiest homicide detective in the city," Troy added, his tone wry.

"My Mac?" Shay asked.

Her Mac, Rory scowled. And didn't that just answer her question right away?

Shay was quiet for a minute. "Well, judging from the way they were eyeing each other way back when, I'd say it's about ten years overdue. A part of me is still slightly jealous that he never looked at me like that."

Like what? "Nothing happened!" Rory protested.

"Maybe, but you both wanted it to," Shay responded. "I think he'd be really good for you."

"He almost cheated on you, with me!" Rory half yelled. Okay, the straws she was grabbing were elusive but she was giving it her best shot.

"He was twenty-four, we were having problems and whenever the two of you were in the same room you created an electrical storm. Besides, as you said, nothing happened. It's not that big a deal."

Shay must've forgotten that being kissed by Mac was a very big deal.

"Go for it, Rorks."

Okay, who was this woman and what had she done with Rory's insecure, neurotic sister? "Are you high?" Rory demanded. "He's a commitment-phobic man-slut! He changes women like he changes socks!"

"I don't think that's true. Not so much and not anymore." Shay laughed. "I liked Mac. I still like Mac. He was a good egg and he put up with an enormous amount of drama from me. You should date him, Rorks, give this relationship thing a spin. Who knows, you might end up being… I don't know…*happy*?"

Troy looked triumphant and Rory placed her hands over her face. "You are high. It's the only explanation…"

"Or that my hot detective husband came home for lunch and, well, let's just say food wasn't a priority," Shay smugly stated.

Troy groaned and Rory let out a strangled *ewww*. Shay disconnected the call on a happy laugh. Rory stared out the window for a long time before turning to Troy. "Do you agree?" she quietly asked him. "Do you think I should take a chance, see where this goes?"

"Do you really love him?"

Rory thought about his question, not wanting to give a glib answer. "I'm worried that it's temporary craziness, that when the fire dies down, I'll run…or he'll run…and someone will get hurt. I'm scared to get hurt."

"Aren't we all?" Troy reached across the seats to grip her fingers in his. "Yeah, it might fail. It might burn out. You might get hurt."

"So encouraging," Rory murmured.

Troy sent her a sweet, sweet smile. "But, honey, what if it doesn't? What if this is the amazing love story you've been waiting for? What if he is the big *it*? What if it works?"

Rory looked at him and slumped in her seat. "Humpf."

Troy laughed, pulled his hand back and then his face turned serious. "Don't run, honey, not this time. Stand still and see what happens. Will you?"

Rory smiled at him and, liking the connection, reached across the seat to link her fingers back into his. "Yeah. I think I will. If—"

Troy groaned. "Oh, God."

Rory ignored his protest "—you will consider borrowing some money from me to move your mom into that home."

Troy sighed. "Diabolical."

Rory's smile was smug. "I try."

Eleven

Mac ran a hand through his hair and unbuttoned the jacket to his gray suit. He took a sip of his whiskey and looked at his watch; Rory was late but that was okay. He needed a moment to himself, to think, even if he had to take that moment while standing in a crowded cocktail bar, surrounded by his friends and colleagues. He sipped again and ignored the pain in his arm—thanks to his session on the ice—and the noise around him, ignored the insults, jokes and crude comments flying over his head. The pain wasn't as bad as he'd thought it would be but he definitely didn't have the power and strength in the limb that he was used to. His teammates had tried to cover for him and he was grateful for their efforts. Hopefully they'd done a good enough job to fool Bayliss.

On the plus side, Mac thought, Rory *had* arrived at the practice. He'd been surprised at the relief he felt, astonished that as soon as he saw her, his heart rate accelerated but his soul settled down.

She was there. Everything was all right in his world. When had that happened? When had she become so important to his emotional well-being that she could calm him with one look, with one sarcastic comment?

If you do any more damage I will personally kick your ass.

It wasn't an "I love you" or "I will support you no matter what," but it was Rory's version of "Okay, this one time, I'll trust you." He could work with that.

God, he *wanted* to work through whatever this was with her. Was it love? He didn't know, but he knew it was *something.* Many women had caught his eye over the years, and he'd slept with quite a few of them—probably more than he should have—but Rory was still the only person who'd come close to capturing his heart.

But…and, hell, there was always a *but*, Mac thought, staring down at the floor between his feet. *But* he didn't know if he could spend the rest of his life reassuring her that he wouldn't cheat, that he wouldn't let her down. He *wouldn't* cheat, but there would come a time when he disappointed her, when he wouldn't be there for her, when things went wrong. Would she bail at the first hint of trouble or would she cut him some slack?

He was a man, one with little experience of this thing called a relationship or how to be in it, and he knew, for sure, that he'd mess up. When he did, and it was a *when* and not an *if*, would she talk it out or would she walk? If she walked, would he be able to stand it? The rational side of him suggested it might be better not to take the chance, to call it quits now before anyone—him—got hurt. That would be the clever, the practical, the smart thing to do.

Except that would mean not having Rory in his life, and he didn't think he could go back to his empty life, hopping from one feminine bed to another. Nor did he think he could become a monk. Both options sucked. Mac scrubbed his hand over his face...

Relationships were so damn complicated and exhausting.

"Mac."

Quinn nudged his elbow into Mac's ribs and Mac turned to look down into the weathered face of Kade's investor. He'd changed into an ugly brown suit and combed his thin hair but he still didn't look like someone who could provide what they needed. *Don't judge a book by its cover*, Mac reminded himself. The granddaughter looked spectacular, Mac noticed, because he was a man and that was what men did. Her bright red hair was pulled back into a low ponytail and her wide eyes darted between him, Kade and Quinn.

Kade cleared his throat. "Mr. Bayliss, meet Mac McCaskill. Mac, Mr. Bayliss and his granddaughter, Wren."

Mac shook the man's hand with its surprisingly strong grip and made the appropriate comments. After they exchanged the usual pleasantries, Kade and Quinn drew Wren into another conversation and Mac tried not to squirm when Bayliss regarded him with a steady, penetrating look. "You've definitely lost power in your arm. Your slap shot was weak and ineffectual."

Hell, Mac had hoped he wouldn't notice. The old man was sharper than he looked. Mac pasted a nothing-to-worry-about expression on his face and shrugged. "I pulled a muscle a while back and this was my first practice. It'll be fine soon. I'm regaining power every day."

"We'll see. I'm not sure if you will ever regain your form."

Mac felt like the old man had sucker-punched him. "That's not something you need to worry about." He forced himself to keep his voice even. "I *will* be back to full strength soon and I *will* lead this team next season."

"We'll see," Bayliss repeated, and Mac wanted to scream. "Luckily, I see enough talent in this team to want to invest whether you are part of it or not, whether you play or not. It was nice meeting you, Mr. McCaskill. We'll talk again."

Mac stared at Bayliss's back as he and Kade walked away, then he forced himself to sip his drink, to look as though he hadn't been slapped.

Whether he played or not? Hell, if he didn't play, what could he do for the team? Kade was the management guy. Despite his youth, Quinn was a damn excellent coach… what did Mac bring to the party apart from his skill on the ice? If playing wasn't an option, there was no way he was going to float around the Mavericks on the outside looking in, making a nuisance of himself. He was either a full partner or not. A full contributor or not.

God, *not*. Was that a possibility?

"Want to dance, Mac?"

He blinked at the perfectly made-up face to his right and couldn't put a name to the gorgeous blonde. He looked toward the entrance, still didn't see Rory and decided what the hell. Dancing was better than standing there like an idiot freaking out over his future. He nodded, handed his glass to a passing waiter and allowed the blonde to lead him to the dance floor. When they reached the small circle, he placed his hands on her hips and wished she was Rory. He could talk to Rory about

the bombshell he'd just experienced, about the fear holding him in its icy grip.

She'd help him make sense of it, Mac thought as his
dance partner moved closer, her breasts brushing his
chest. He felt nothing, no corresponding flash of desire
and no interest down south. Huh, so if things didn't work
out with Rory it looked like he'd be going the monk route.

He tried to put some distance between them but the
dance floor was crowded and there was little room to
move. Mac sighed when she laid her head on his shoulder. She didn't feel right, smell right; she was too tall, too
buxom, too curvy…where the hell was Rory?

Over the heads of most of his fellow dancers he looked
toward the door and there she was, dressed in a scarlet
cocktail dress he wanted to rip off with his teeth. She had
a small bag clutched under her arm and she was holding
her cell phone… She was here, *finally*, and all was well
with his world.

Then he lifted his eyes back up to hers and his heart
plummeted at the expression on her face. Her eyes were
huge and wide, her skin pale and she looked like she'd
been slapped. Even from a distance he could tell her eyes
were full of tears and her bottom lip trembled. *Oh, crap…*

He wanted to yell that her addition sucked. Two plus
two did not equal seventeen! He was just dancing with
the woman, not doing her on the dance floor. He hadn't
given his dance partner one thought; in fact, he'd been
desperately waiting for Rory to arrive to rescue him…

One dance and the accusations, as sure as sugar, were
flying, silent and deadly. He could read her thoughts as
clearly as if she'd bellowed them across the room. *I can't
trust you. You've let me down. You've disappointed me.*

The voices in his head mocked him. Hell, even his mother's voice came to join the suck-fest.

You'll never be quite good enough. This is why you should keep your distance. This hurt is gonna be your constant companion for the rest of your life. You don't deserve normal and you sure as hell don't deserve love... She doesn't trust you. She never will. You always manage to mess it up...

The expression on Rory's face put it all into perspective. They'd been back together for a day, sort of, and with one dance with a complete stranger, he'd been unfairly fouled. And if that wasn't life telling him this would never work then he didn't know what was.

Rory looked down at her phone, lifted it to her ear and bit her lip. She sent him another look, one he couldn't quite interpret, spun on her heel and left the room. She was running as hard and as fast as she could. Mentally, emotionally and, dammit, literally.

That was that, Mac thought, walking off the dance floor toward the bar. He felt like he was carrying a fifty-pound anvil around in his chest instead of a heart. Since he wasn't about to have sex in the near future and he might be saying goodbye to his career with the Mavericks, he might as well have a drink.

Or many.

Rory sat next to Troy's bed, holding his hand and willing him to wake up. She'd been at his bedside for twelve hours straight and he was still unconscious. Rory looked at his medical chart at the end of his bed and told herself there was no point in reading it again, it wouldn't change the facts.

Troy, on his way to start his evening shift at The

Annex next door, had failed to stop at a traffic light and plowed his rust bucket into the side of a truck. He'd smacked his head on the steering wheel and had swelling on the brain. When the swelling subsided they would reevaluate his condition.

That damn car, Rory thought, placing her forehead on his cold wrist. Guess the car service hadn't included checking the brakes. The car was a write-off, Rory had been told by the paramedics; it was their opinion that he'd been lucky to escape alive.

Rory shuddered. Troy was her best friend and she couldn't imagine her life without him. And speaking of people who were important to her, where the hell was Mac? She'd risked using her cell in the ICU and left two brief, urgent, *desperate* messages on his cell for him to call her but he'd yet to respond. Why not? Why was he ignoring her? What had changed?

Sure she'd seen him dancing with that blonde but that didn't worry her. Anyone with a brain in her head would've noticed that it had been the blonde making all the moves. Mac had been supremely disinterested. In fact, despite the devastating news she'd just received about Troy—one of the nurses in the ER had texted her as soon as he was rushed in—she'd immediately noticed Mac looked distracted, worried. His eyes were bleak and that telltale muscle in his jaw was jumping.

Was this what their life would be like going forward, Rory wondered? Her being pushed down his priority list because there was something more important he needed to do, somewhere more interesting he needed to be? Could she cope with playing second fiddle to his career, his friends, his teammates? She'd done that with her father and she'd hated every moment.

She couldn't do that, not again. She loved Mac with everything she had but she wouldn't sacrifice herself for him, for any man. She didn't expect him to jump hurdles when she asked for any little thing, but Troy's critical condition was pretty mammoth. She had a right to ask Mac for his emotional support, to be there for her. At the very least, he could reply to her damn messages!

Damn, life had been so uncomplicated when she'd been unattached. Boring, but simple.

Mac, sitting on the couch in Kade's office, propped his feet onto the coffee table and stared at the massive photograph on Kade's wall. It was of the team, naturally, minutes after the final whistle of the Stanley Cup Final. He and Quinn and Kade had their arms around each other, all of them wearing face-splitting grins. Would he ever be that happy again, Mac wondered?

"How long are you going to sit over there and stare moodily at my wall?" Kade asked, replacing the handset of his desk phone into its cradle. "'Cause I've got to tell you, it's getting old."

Mac lifted a lazy middle finger and kept staring at the photograph. "That was a really good day at the office."

Kade's eyes flicked to the photograph. "It was. Now are you going to sit here and reminisce about the past or are you going to tell me what's got your lacy panties in a twist?"

Mac pulled a face. Over the past four days he'd been avoiding his friends to spend his days on his balcony staring out at the view, and he was, frankly, tired of himself and his woe-is-me attitude.

Rory and he were kaput. Admittedly, she had left two messages on his voice mail the night she bolted from the bar, which he'd ignored. Really, what was there to say? She either trusted him or she didn't, and it was clear that she didn't.

There was no point in discussing the issue.

Game over. Move on.

"Anymore news from the Bayliss camp?" Mac asked, dropping his feet to the floor and reaching for the bottle of water he'd placed on the coffee table.

Kade leaned back in his chair. "I'm expecting to see the first draft of an agreement today."

Even if Mac wasn't part of the day-to-day equation he'd be a part owner, and he was glad to see progress. At least with Kade and Quinn at the helm the Mavericks would have a good chance of keeping their identity. "That's good news."

Kade shrugged. "We'll see what the document contains. I know that Wren, the granddaughter and a PR specialist, has some strong ideas about what she wants to happen with the franchise."

Mac rubbed his jaw, thick with stubble. "Yeah, I don't think I'm part of those franchise plans."

Kade frowned at him. "What do you mean?"

"Didn't you hear what Bayliss said the other night?" When Kade shook his head, Mac explained, "He noticed that my arm was weak and expressed doubts as to whether I would still have a place on the Mavericks next season."

Kade narrowed his eyes. "That will never be his decision to make." His eyes radiated hot frustration even though his voice was calm. "He's providing marketing and merchandising opportunities, access to bigger sponsorship deals, connections. He will not be allowed to interfere with the team and its selection."

"Yeah, I don't think he got that memo," Mac replied in his driest voice. He took a deep breath and bit his lip. "If I, and my injury, become a point of contention, I'll back off. If it means keeping the team out of the clutches of that soul-sucking corporation then I'll be a silent partner."

Kade rolled his eyes. "Shut the hell up, McCaskill, you suck as a martyr. You will be back, at full strength, by the time the season starts or I will kick your ass. And I can still do it," Kade warned him.

"You can try." Mac stood up and crossed to the floor-to-ceiling windows. When he turned back to Kade his expression was serious. "We should think of a plan B, just in case I'm not."

"Rory told me you've made excellent progress."

Mac shrugged. He had, but it would take a lot more work, and he'd keep at it. He'd keep pushing himself but Rory wouldn't be there to monitor his progress, to keep him in check. The chances were high that he'd push himself too hard and do some serious damage. Or, because he was scared to make the situation worse, he wouldn't do enough.

Funny how he'd work his ass off for his arm but not for his heart.

Mac jerked at the thought and felt like a million lightbulbs had switched on in his head. Where had that thought come from? Did it really matter? The truth was the truth…and what he was thinking about his arm should apply to his life, as well. He and Rory had started something ten years ago, and because they were young, and dumb, they'd walked away from it not recognizing what it actually was.

A connection, a future, safety. She'd always been what he'd needed, what his soul needed.

Either way, without her, he was screwed. He was screwed anyway; his arm ached, his heart ached. He was thoroughly miserable. He wanted to see her. He needed to see her. He needed to see if she also thought they had something worthwhile, a connection worth working *on*. There was a good possibility she'd say no but he was willing to take the risk, to do the work. Nothing worth achieving came easy and if he failed, yeah it would suck but he refused to live with regret. He knew what he wanted and was prepared to work his ass off to get it.

He wanted Rory.

And if he failed to win her, he'd survive. He always did.

But he had no intention of failing. Because anything was better than this Rory-shaped emptiness inside him.

He belted toward the door, tossing a "Later" over his shoulder and ignoring the deeply sarcastic "Good chat" that drifted out of Kade's office.

Five days after his accident Troy finally opened his eyes. Three hours after that, when he started arguing with his nurse, Rory realized she could leave him. She could go home to her own bed and have a decent night's sleep. She could spend more than a couple of hours in her apartment, eat something other than fast food, cut down on her coffee.

Leaving Troy and the nurse to bicker, she walked out of his room. Once she was in the hallway, she placed her forearm against the nearest wall and buried her face in the crook of her elbow. Troy was going to be fine. She could stop worrying and start thinking about something other than planning his funeral. Rory felt the tears track down her face and thought how ridiculous it was that she was crying now, when he was finally out of danger, when it was all but over.

Intellectually she knew her reaction was because she could finally relax. She could stop the continuous praying, the bargaining with God. Stupid, but human nature, she thought. Saints alive, she was so tired.

Rory recognized the big hands on her hips and sighed when Mac gently turned her around. Through her tears she noticed his gentle, compassionate expression, the tenderness in his eyes. Even though she was mad at him— he'd certainly taken his time getting here!—she was still ridiculously glad to see him. Her throat tightened as the strength of her tears increased. She felt like she would shatter from the effort it took to not fling herself against his chest and burrow into his warmth.

He took the decision from her by sliding his big hand around the back of her neck and pulling her to his chest. Her arms, shaky with exhaustion, slid around his waist. His other arm held her as her knees buckled.

"It's okay, honey. I've got you," he said in her ear. "I've got you and I'm not letting you go."

She wished she could believe him but she was so fatigued, so emotionally drained she couldn't think. All she knew was that Mac was finally here and she could rest. So she did. Rory wasn't sure how long she stood in his arms. All she knew was that he was strong and solid and *there*. She wasn't alone.

When she'd regained some of her equilibrium, she stepped back, dashed a hand against her wet cheeks and stared at his hard chest. "How did you know I was here?" she asked in a brittle voice. Her tears, it seemed, were still very close to the surface.

Mac pushed her hair off her forehead. "Well, since

your phone has been off and you weren't at your apartment, I started to get worried. So I called Shay and asked about you."

"And she told you I was here?"

"Mmm, after coercing season tickets out of me," Mac said on a small smile that quickly died. "You should've told me about Troy. Why didn't you?"

Rory wasn't so tired that she couldn't react to that. "I thought my rushing from that bar was a good enough hint that something was drastically wrong! And you could've returned my messages!"

"I thought you were running from me because you saw me dancing with that blonde."

"She wasn't worth worrying about. No, I'd just heard about Troy."

Mac closed his eyes in obvious frustration. "I am such an idiot."

"No arguments from me," Rory said, stepping out of his reach. She gestured to Troy's door. "Troy had an accident. It was touch and go for a while."

"I know. Shay told me. She also told me you've spent every minute of the day with him since it happened."

Rory rubbed the back of her neck. "Not every minute. I went home to shower."

"He doesn't have any family?" Mac closed the distance between them.

"Only a mother who has dementia. That's why Troy was driving a crappy car, all his spare cash goes to her nursing home fees."

Mac's hand drew circles on her back and she had to restrain herself from purring like a cat. Rory, knowing how his touch could relax her and tempt her to forgive him too easily, snapped her spine straight. "Anyway, why are you here? I suppose you've been worried about your physio sessions." She tried to sound breezy but it didn't come out that way. "Sorry about that."

Mac's smile was one she'd never seen before, a combination of tenderness, protectiveness and love. It scared the hell out of her.

"Look, I'd appreciate it if you gave me a day to get some rest and then we can get back on track and schedule some sessions. Have you been doing your exercises?" she demanded.

Mac shook his head and bent his knees so they were eye to eye. "Rory?"

"Yes?"

"Shut up for a sec, okay?" Mac waited to see whether she would talk again, and when she didn't, he nodded his satisfaction. "So this is what is going to happen—I'm taking you back to my place and you're going to stand, or sit, in my shower until you are pink and boneless. Then you are going to eat something, soup maybe, and then we are going to climb into bed where you will sleep in my arms. Got it?"

"Uh…" She was beyond tired. She couldn't even find the energy to respond, let alone argue.

"Just say yes."

Rory nodded as tears welled again. "Excellent." Mac wound his arm around her shoulders and walked her down the passage toward the exit. "I like it when I get to boss you around," he teased.

Rory wasn't too tired to allow him to get away with that comment. "Don't get used to it, McCaskill. It's only because I'm exhausted."

Rory opened her lids and squinted in the bright sunlight stabbing her eyes. She placed her arm in front of her face to cut out the glare, looking out from under her arm across the pale floorboards to the partially open doors that led to a balcony.

A pair of very large sneakers were on the floor and a T-shirt, one she didn't recognize, was draped over the back of a black bucket chair. Through the open doors she saw a pair of bare feet up on a wrought-iron table, perilously close to a carafe of coffee.

Coffee. She'd kill for some. Rory sat up, looked down and couldn't help noticing she was naked. Casting her mind back, she remembered Mac carrying her up the stairs to his bedroom, stripping her down and pushing her into bed. She had a vague recollection of a warm body wrapped around hers as she fell asleep. Clasping the sheet to her chest, she sat up and pushed her hair out of her eyes, running her tongue over her teeth.

Coffee or a toothbrush? Either would do nicely right now.

"You look good in my bed."

Rory turned her head to see Mac standing in the doorway leading in from the balcony wearing a pair of straight-legged track pants and a black T-shirt. His hair was messed and his beard was about three days past stubble and she thought he was the sexiest creature she'd ever laid eyes on.

"Hi," she said, self-conscious.

"Hi back," Mac replied on a smile. "You're looking better, thank God. You scared me…you were totally out of it."

"I felt shell-shocked," Rory admitted, looking around. "Can you pass me something to wear?"

"Why? I rather like you naked," Mac replied, teasing. He picked up the black T-shirt that lay across his chair and held it up. "I did a load of laundry earlier and I tossed your clothes in too. Will this do?"

"You can do laundry?" Rory asked, amused as she caught the T-shirt he tossed her way.

"I can do lots of things," Mac replied, his voice quieter. "Would you like some coffee?"

Rory nodded and watched as he walked back out onto the balcony and returned with a cup of coffee, which he handed over. Rory took a sip and quickly realized it was barely warm but strong enough to put scales on her chest. Okay, so Mac wasn't as together as he sounded, she thought. Very good to know that she wasn't the only one in the room wondering what she was doing here.

What *was* she doing here?

Mac sat on the edge of the bed, his bended knee touching her thigh. He stared down at the floor, and when he spoke, his voice vibrated with emotion. "I once told you that hockey is everything to me, that it was the highest priority in my life."

"Mmm-hmm?"

"It has been my life for the past fifteen years. It's afforded me this amazing lifestyle and I've loved every moment I've spent on and off the ice."

Okay, he wasn't telling her anything new here.

"I love you more."

Rory's mouth fell open. Had he really said what she thought he'd said? She needed to make sure. "Say that again?"

"You are the highest priority in my life. You make it better, brighter and more fun." Mac sent her an uncertain look and his hand gripped her thigh covered by the sheet. "Look, I know I screwed up. I know you needed me, and I let my insecurities get the best of me. I hate that I let you down. I want to do better. I *will* do better. And I know you have trust issues too. You say you don't do relationships but I'd like us to try.

"Before you say no let me say this—I will never cheat on you, I promise. Actually, the closest I've ever come to cheating was that kiss we shared. I've never been involved with anyone deeply enough for this to be an issue but, in my defense, I've always ended one affair before I started another."

"Um…okay?"

"But you aren't an affair. You are the only person I can be real with. Someone I can really talk to… You are my best friend. I'm sorry I wasn't there for you. I want to make it up to you. I'll spend my whole life making it up to you, if you'll let me."

Rory placed her hand over her heart, her lower lip trembling as she listened to this innately masculine man humble himself before her.

"Give me a shot, Rory. Give *us* a shot," Mac pleaded, emotion radiating from his eyes.

"What if we fail, Mac?" she asked in a quiet voice.

"Aw, baby…" Mac blew out a breath and shrugged. "I don't fail and you're too important to me to let that happen. But if we do, then we'll go down knowing we gave it our best, knowing we loved rather than living a half-life, guarding our hearts and thoughts and emotions."

"You make it sound so easy," Rory whispered.

"It'll be anything but easy," Mac replied. "It'll be tough, and we'll fight and we'll sometimes wonder what the hell we were thinking. But through it all we'll love each other." Mac pushed an agitated hand through his hair. "We'll have to spend time apart when I'm on the road. But you'll have your own practice to keep you busy and we'll talk every night and text every hour. We'll spend every minute we can together and we'll work at it, dammit, because the one thing we are both good at is hard work, Rorks. If we work at loving each other as hard as we do at everything else, we can't do anything but succeed."

It was a compelling argument, Rory thought, wishing she could throw her fear aside and launch herself into his arms, into their future. "I'm scared, Mac."

"So am I." Mac leaned forward and rested his forehead against hers. "We can be scared together. Do you think you can love me, Rorks? Some day and at some stage?"

Rory pulled her head back, astounded at his comment. She placed a hand on his chest. "You think I don't love you?"

"Well, you haven't exactly uttered the words," Mac said conversationally, but she could feel his galloping heartbeat under her hand.

Rory linked her arms around his neck and looked into his eyes. "I do love you. I think I fell in love with you the first time you almost kissed me." Rory placed her forehead against his temple. "I thought I was going to be alone forever but I can't be. It's no longer who I am, who I've become by knowing you. Who I am now is someone who loves you—now, tomorrow, forever. I might have had a hand in rehabilitating your arm but you rehabilitated my heart."

Mac's hand on her neck tightened in response. "Oh, Rorks, you slay me. So, we agree that we love each other and this is it?"

"I so agree to that."

"Excellent." Mac grinned. "Now, let's move on to another important issue…"

Rory lifted her eyebrows as he pulled his T-shirt over his head. "I think we've covered the high points."

Mac dropped a hard, openmouthed kiss on her lips before lifting her shirt up and over her head. "Getting you naked is always going to be very high on my agenda."

Rory curled her hand around his neck as he pushed her back into the pillows. His eyes were soft as they connected with hers. He swallowed, started to speak, cleared his throat and tried again. "Everything that is most important to me is here, right now. I'm holding my world in my arms," Mac said, his tone low and soaked with tenderness. "It feels good."

"It feels amazing," Rory replied, her voice cracking with emotion. Blinking her tears away, she lifted her hips and wiggled. Her smile turned naughty as her hand drifted down his back to rest on one very fine butt cheek. "*You* feel amazing. So, McCaskill, are you going to kiss me or what?"

Mac grinned. "Oh, yeah. Anytime, anywhere— *everywhere*—for the rest of your life. Starting right now…"

* * * * *

REQUEST YOUR FREE BOOKS!
2 FREE NOVELS PLUS 2 FREE GIFTS!

ⓗ HARLEQUIN®

Desire

ALWAYS POWERFUL, PASSIONATE AND PROVOCATIVE

YES! Please send me 2 FREE Harlequin® Desire novels and my 2 FREE gifts (gifts are worth about $10). After receiving them, if I don't wish to receive any more books, I can return the shipping statement marked "cancel." If I don't cancel, I will receive 6 brand-new novels every month and be billed just $4.55 per book in the U.S. or $5.24 per book in Canada. That's a savings of at least 13% off the cover price! It's quite a bargain! Shipping and handling is just 50¢ per book in the U.S. and 75¢ per book in Canada.* I understand that accepting the 2 free books and gifts places me under no obligation to buy anything. I can always return a shipment and cancel at any time. Even if I never buy another book, the two free books and gifts are mine to keep forever.

225/326 HDN GH2P

Name _____ (PLEASE PRINT)

Address _____ Apt. #

City _____ State/Prov. _____ Zip/Postal Code

Signature (if under 18, a parent or guardian must sign)

Mail to the **Reader Service:**
IN U.S.A.: P.O. Box 1867, Buffalo, NY 14240-1867
IN CANADA: P.O. Box 609, Fort Erie, Ontario L2A 5X3

Want to try two free books from another line?
Call 1-800-873-8635 or visit www.ReaderService.com.

* Terms and prices subject to change without notice. Prices do not include applicable taxes. Sales tax applicable in N.Y. Canadian residents will be charged applicable taxes. Offer not valid in Quebec. This offer is limited to one order per household. Not valid for current subscribers to Harlequin Desire books. All orders subject to credit approval. Credit or debit balances in a customer's account(s) may be offset by any other outstanding balance owed by or to the customer. Please allow 4 to 6 weeks for delivery. Offer available while quantities last.

Your Privacy—The Reader Service is committed to protecting your privacy. Our Privacy Policy is available online at www.ReaderService.com or upon request from the Reader Service.

We make a portion of our mailing list available to reputable third parties that offer products we believe may interest you. If you prefer that we not exchange your name with third parties, or if you wish to clarify or modify your communication preferences, please visit us at www.ReaderService.com/consumerschoice or write to us at Reader Service Preference Service, P.O. Box 9062, Buffalo, NY 14240-9062. Include your complete name and address.

HDI5

With CEO Carson Newport and his top employee, PR director Georgia Adams, spending long hours together at the office, the line between business and pleasure blurs. But his family's scandals may challenge everything he knows and unravel the affair they've begun...

Read on for a sneak peek at
SAYING YES TO THE BOSS
the latest installment in the
DYNASTIES: THE NEWPORTS series
by Andrea Laurence.

"To the new Cynthia Newport Memorial Hospital for Children!" Carson said, holding up his glass. "I really can't believe we're making this happen." Setting down his cup, he wrapped Georgia in his arms and spun her around.

"Carson!" Georgia squealed and clung to his neck.

When he finally set her back on the ground, both of them were giggling and giddy from drinking the champagne on empty stomachs. Georgia stumbled dizzily against his chest and held on to his shoulders.

"Thank you for finding this," he said.

"I know it's important to you," she said, noting he still had his arms around her waist. Carson was the leanest of his brothers, but his grip on her told of hard muscles hidden beneath his expensive suit.

In that moment, the giggles ceased and they were staring intently into each other's eyes. Carson's full lips were only inches from hers. She could feel his warm breath brushing over her skin. She'd imagined standing like this with him so many times, and every one of those times, he'd kissed her.

Before she knew what was happening, Carson pressed his lips to hers. The champagne was just strong enough to mute the voices in her head that told her this was a bad idea. Instead she pulled him closer.

He tasted like champagne and spearmint. His touch was gentle yet firm. She could've stayed just like this forever, but eventually, Carson pulled away.

For a moment, Georgia felt light-headed. She didn't know if it was his kiss or the champagne, but she felt as though she would lift right off the ground if she let go. Then she looked up at him.

His green eyes reflected sudden panic. Her emotions came crashing back down to the ground with the reality she saw there. She had just kissed her boss. Her boss! And despite the fact that he had initiated it, he looked just as horrified by the idea.

"Georgia, I…" he started, his voice trailing off. "I didn't mean for that to happen."

With a quick shake of her head, she dismissed his words and took a step back from him. "Don't worry about it," she said. "Excitement and champagne will make people do stupid things every time."

The problem was that it hadn't felt stupid. It had felt amazing.

Don't miss a single story in Dynasties: The Newports
Passion and chaos consume a Chicago real estate empire

SAYING YES TO THE BOSS
by Andrea Laurence, available July 2016!

And
AN HEIR FOR THE BILLIONAIRE by Kat Cantrell
CLAIMED BY THE COWBOY by Sarah M. Anderson
HIS SECRET BABY BOMBSHELL by Jules Bennett
BACK IN THE ENEMY'S BED by Michelle Celmer
THE TEXAN'S ONE NIGHT STAND-OFF by Charlene Sands
Coming soon!

www.Harlequin.com

HDEXP0616

Whatever You're Into… Passionate Reads

Looking for more passionate reads from Harlequin®?
Fear not! Harlequin® Presents, Harlequin® Desire and
Harlequin® Blaze offer you irresistible romance stories
featuring powerful heroes.

◆HARLEQUIN *Presents.*

Do you want alpha males, decadent glamour and jet-set
lifestyles? Step into the sensational, sophisticated world of
Harlequin® Presents, where sinfully tempting heroes ignite a
fierce and wickedly irresistible passion!

◆HARLEQUIN *Desire*

Harlequin® Desire novels are powerful, passionate and
provocative contemporary romances set against a backdrop of
wealth, privilege and sweeping family saga. Alpha heroes with
a soft side meet strong-willed but vulnerable heroines amid a
dramatic world of divided loyalties, high-stakes conflict and
intense emotion.

◆HARLEQUIN *Blaze*

Harlequin® Blaze stories sizzle with strong heroines and
irresistible heroes playing the game of modern love and lust.
They're fun, sexy and always steamy.

Be sure to check out our full selection of books
within each series every month!

www.Harlequin.com

HPASSION2016